...dent Foreign Fiction Prize and the Jewish Quarterly Fiction Prize, and *Good Intentions* (2002) and *Chez Moi* (2008). *The Foundling* was awarded the Prix Renaudot des Lycéens on publication in France. www.agnesdesarthe.com

ADRIANA HUNTER has been working as a literary translator since 1998, and has now translated nearly 50 books from the French, including the novels mentioned above and, for Portobello Books, Véronique Ovaldé's *Kick the Animal Out* (a finalist for the French-American Foundation and the Florence Gould Foundation Translation Prize) and *And My See-Through Heart*. She won the Scott Moncrieff Prize for her translation of Véronique Olmi's *Beside the Sea*. She has three children and lives in Norfolk.

Also by Agnès Desarthe from Portobello Books

Chez Moi

THE
Foundling

Agnès Desarthe

Translated from the French by Adriana Hunter

First published by Portobello Books 2012
Paperback edition published 2013

Portobello Books
12 Addison Avenue
London
W11 4QR
United Kingdom

A CIP catalogue record for this book is available from the British Library

9 8 7 6 5 4 3 2 1

ISBN 978 1 84627 412 1

www.portobellobooks.com

Typeset in Garamond MT by
Avon DataSet Ltd, Bidford on Avon, Warwickshire
Printed and bound by CPI Group (UK) Ltd, Croydon, CR0 4YY

'A fireball cartwheeling right across the road, then, suddenly, after the bend, blat! Into a tree. This fireball smashes into the trunk and burns the lot, leaves, branches, even the roots. I thought it was like some paranormal phenomenon. But actually it was the boy. The boy on his motorbike. Apparently that don't never happen, bikes catching fire like that, for no reason, but it happened then. I was there. I watched it from above, from the bridge over the main road. That's where I saw it. A fireball.'

Jerome is re-reading the eye-witness account in the local paper. His hands are shaking. His stomach too. He reads it yet again, wonders why the journalist didn't 'massage' the words of this Yvette Réhurdon, farm labourer. For a moment he manages to take his mind off it by imagining the editors' meeting during which they agreed to transcribe, verbatim, the words recorded onto a pocket tape recorder by the primary school teacher who writes their news-in-brief column in her spare time.

Almost immediately the trembling, which had subsided, starts up again. Jerome wants to cry, he thinks it would be a release, but his tears won't come. The boy wasn't his son, he was his daughter's sweetheart.

Is that what you say, sweetheart? He doesn't know. How did Marina put it? My boyfriend? No. She said Armand.

Jerome is sitting in the living room and, through his daughter's closed bedroom door, he can hear sobs, moans, occasionally a cry. He has no idea what he is supposed to do.

Before leaving for work this morning he went to see her. He turned the handle very softly, so as not to wake her, just in case. But she was not asleep. She was lying on her front, crying. He went over to her.

He thought he might stroke her shoulder. But when Marina heard him, she looked up. Jerome saw her face and fled.

It's completely natural for her to resent me, he thought. Why isn't it me who's dead? That would be easier. That would be normal.

Jerome is fifty-six years old. And the boy, how old was he? Eighteen, like Marina? Maybe nineteen.

Armand.

Such a pretty sounding name, Armand.

Jerome fiddles with the fish-shaped placemat in the middle of the table while his thoughts wander. He puts the newspaper down. He would like to read the account of the accident once more. He daren't. What's the point? There was nothing left of the boy. A boot buckle, perhaps. The zip from his jacket.

Jerome thinks of Edith Piaf's song about a man on a motorbike in a leather jacket. Hates himself for being so easily distracted. He wishes he could be submerged in grief, inhabiting it, like Marina. But his mind gallivants around. He comes up with all sorts of rubbish. Perhaps, he thinks, if he reads the interview with Yvette Réhurdon, farm labourer, enough times, he will eventually manage to concentrate.

Why bother? He doesn't know. He feels he is expected to give some sort of reaction. But what sort? And who is expecting it? Who is waiting for him to react? He has been living alone with Marina since Paula left him. That was four years ago.

Paula, that was a pretty name too, Jerome says to himself.

He loathes being in this state. Mawkish and aimless. But he can't do anything about it. He feels he is no longer in control. He is coasting. Death has that effect. It's very powerful, death.

No. I really can't be thinking crap like that, he tells himself. But he is. That's exactly what he's thinking, that death is powerful. He thinks it with the same intensity as when, three seconds ago, he thought Paula was a pretty name. Paula was also a pretty woman. He still doesn't understand why she married him.

If she were here, she would know exactly how to handle this. She would run her daughter a bath, talk to her, give her a hand massage. She would let fresh air in through the window. Tell her all sorts of twaddle about the soul, about memories we hold inside us forever which give us strength, and about life which picks us all up again eventually.

Jerome admires her. How does she do it?

He always felt that Paula had unravelled the great mystery of... all the great mysteries, in fact. After the separation she bought herself a cottage in a picturesque village in the south. With a big lavender bush and a wisteria in the courtyard. She drinks rosé with her neighbours at sunset. He sometimes thinks about her, and the life she has made for herself a long way away from him. A successful, harmonious life. Through the grey days, and the weeks when the thermometer doesn't get above minus five, he dreams of joining her. On the weather report in the evenings, he looks at the map of France, and there is almost always a sun over where Paula lives, while where they live, he and Marina, it's all freezing fog, morning mists and unsettled periods brought on by a low front from the north-east.

What are they doing here? Why didn't Marina leave with her mother when they separated? You would expect a daughter to go with her mother. He doesn't remember discussing it, not with either of them. And all at once it comes to him: Armand. He and Marina must have been at school together. She was only little, but she was already in love. Marina didn't choose between her mother and her father. Marina chose love. Jerome is sure of it. Yet he only recently discovered the boy existed. Marina is a discreet young woman. She had never brought anyone to the house, then one day, six months ago, she said she wanted to ask someone to supper.

'I'll do the cooking,' she offered. 'I'll do a roast.'

And in the red of her cheeks and the 'o' of that roast, Jerome could tell. He could tell without really knowing. He didn't say to himself my daughter's got a lover, or she wants to introduce me to the boy she loves. He didn't say anything to himself. His thoughts don't produce sentences. They stop just short.

The bell rang at eight thirty. Jerome went to open the door. There was the boy, bottle in hand. Jerome remembers thinking he was tall. He had to look up to his face. What a good-looking boy. His skin... his cheeks... his thick dark eyelashes, the sparkle in his eyes...

Jerome is crying. He puts his head in his hands, for the space of two sobs. One for the bottle of wine in the boy's hands, the other for his good looks.

Then it stops. No more tears. No more images.

The church clock strikes. Jerome stands up and looks out of the window. The hill dropping away outside, the road down below, right at the bottom, and the other hillside beyond, going up to the woods. The rows of russet-coloured vines, the bare earth between their gnarled feet. The sun in the white sky. Sap freezing inside plants. Some tiny little purple flowers have opened in the shadow of the holly hedge. Jerome looks at them and thinks how Armand will never see them.

He remembers reading in some book about people putting bottle ends over the eyes of the dead before laying them in their coffins. He doesn't remember the book's title. Was it a novel? Maybe just a newspaper article. He can't remember, but he likes the idea. These eyes will see no more. Or only through bottle glass. Paradise is so far away, so high up, that you need a magnifying glass to see the earth.

Jerome wonders whether he should go to the funeral. Meet the in-laws who will never be in-laws. He feels awkward and shy. He's afraid. He doesn't know how you shake the hand of a bereaved parent. The physical contact strikes him as sacrilegious. I would never dare, he thinks.

The telephone rings. It is Paula.

'How are you, big boy?' she asks him.

Jerome's heart swells in his chest. A hot air balloon between his diaphragm and his collar bones. I love you. I love you. I love you. That's what he wishes he could say to his ex-wife, for whom he has only ever had modest feelings. Instead, he replies:

'Not great.'

'How about Marina?'

Jerome says nothing. Not a single word comes to him.

'I'm so fucking stupid,' Paula blurts. 'Sorry, I'm so sorry. The funeral's tomorrow, isn't it? I'll catch a plane and then the last train this evening. I'll get there late. Can I sleep at the house? No, that's not a good idea.'

'Yes, yes, it's a very good idea. I'll leave the door unlocked.'

'You are kind.'

'It's only natural.'

'It's awful.'

'Yes.'

'What exactly happened?'

'I don't know. No one knows. The bike caught fire. No one knows why, or how. Apparently he hadn't been drinking.'

'How will anyone ever know?'

'There's no way of knowing.'

'What sort of boy was he?'

'Perfect.'

Jerome is surprised by his own answer. Paula falls silent. She feels swindled. She never met her daughter's perfect boyfriend. She herself has only ever had awkward relationships. Her marriage? Nice, that was the word she most often used to describe it. As if to rub salt in her wounds, Jerome adds:

'I've never seen anything like it. A… how can I put it?… a connection… a… you see, when they were together…'

'Don't do this to me, big boy. Don't do it.'

She hangs up just as he is saying 'lots of love'. He thinks of ringing her back just to say it, to say 'lots of love'. As if it were important, as if their lives depended on it, world stability, justice.

I'm going gaga, he thinks, and smiles, because of the word, and the way he cradles the phone in his hand, like a frog, a mouse. A pleasant feeling suffuses him, a warmth, a very slight euphoria. For a moment he forgot Armand's death because, instead of thinking about the catastrophe, he thought of woodland animals, the sort you come across on a walk, and catching their eye feels secret, furtive, incomparable. It was just a reprieve. His smile falls apart. He goes over to the door. Whoever it is has rung three times now.

Through the frosted glass he recognises Rosy's silhouette. Rosy has always been fat. She and Marina have been best friends since nursery school. She has huge cheeks, like high Manchurian plateaux, Jerome thinks. He doesn't know why Rosy has always been associated with the word 'Manchurian' in his mind, perhaps because of her very dark, slightly slanting eyes, her small flat nose and her pony-like quality.

'Hi, Jerome,' she says, offering her unbelievable cheeks for a kiss.

'Hi, Rosy,' he replies, giving her a hug.

They hold the embrace for a moment, clumsily rubbing each other's backs, then pull apart abruptly, embarrassed.

'It's good of you to come.'

'Of course I would. How is she? I've brought her schoolwork.'

'Oh, well, you know, I don't think…'

'No really,' says Rosy very confidently as she sets off down the corridor, her huge body swaying from one leg to the other. 'Mustn't let go. Mustn't let anything go.'

How does she know? Jerome wonders.

He watches her heading for the bedroom door.

He can still see them, her and Marina, when they were seven years old. One resting her head on the other's stomach and saying, 'I love you because you're comfortable,' and the other replying, 'I love you because you always say nice things.' He thinks these are both very good reasons for loving someone.

When the door opens, the din Marina's making pervades the house. It is violent as a blast of wind. Jerome's hands fly instinctively to his ears. This noise must stop. But the moment he is aware of his gesture, he orders his arms to drop back down. This is his child crying, not the idiot next door trimming his hedge.

Rosy doesn't lose heart, she goes in and closes the door behind her. The sound level drops immediately. Jerome takes a few steps down the corridor, and listens. He hears Rosy's voice. Then crying. Rosy's voice again. Then nothing. Rosy's voice singing a song in English. A deluge of sobs, gulps, a wail, sobs, several cries. Rosy is still singing. The crying stops. Rosy sings.

Louder and louder. All of a sudden the door opens. Rosy catches Jerome with his ear almost flat against the wall.

'I know this is a non-smoking house, Jerome. I completely respect that. But this is a bit of an exception. I think we need to smoke. I wanted to ask your permission. If we open the window?'

Jerome shrugs his shoulders, nods his head. Right now he would give anything to be able to smoke too. He has never touched a cigarette in his life. What a mistake! He should have started at fifteen like everyone else. If he hadn't wanted to be all different, he could offer them one now, smoke with them – as Indians would a peace pipe – without a word. Not needing to talk to be together.

'No probs,' he says, because he heard a teenager say it a couple of days ago in the car park by the post office.

Rosy smiles at him, more Manchurian than ever, and closes the door again.

The stupid expression he has just used lingers in the house. Jerome goes into the kitchen and 'no probs' follows him. He opens a cupboard to make himself a coffee and 'no probs' pops out. He goes back into the corridor in the hope that the crying will drown out its persistent echo, but there isn't a single sound coming from his daughter's bedroom now. This is the silence of a smoking session, the infinite calm of inhalation. 'No probs' bounces from one wall to the other along the corridor. Jerome hurries into the living room, unfolds the sofa bed, making all the springs creak, launches himself at the cupboard, throws it wide open, takes out a sheet, a blanket and pillows, and starts making up the bed like a chambermaid possessed by the Devil. He is sweating. He would like to make a lot more noise, but the fabrics slither and mould against each other mutely. Jerome can hear only the internal hubbub of his own body, heartbeats and the click of joints. 'No probs.' Luckily, Rosy starts singing again. She has a lovely voice, both high and rich. He doesn't recognise the tune, a sad, heartbreaking melody. He would never have thought of that: singing a sad song to his weeping daughter. And yet it seems to be working: since Rosy arrived, Marina has stopped crying.

Jerome contemplates the bed he has made for Paula: white sheets, cream-coloured mohair. He thinks it looks cosy, much more inviting than his own, which is covered with a hideous multicoloured duvet. Until today, he never thought his room was ugly. He never thinks about sheets, dusters and towels. He couldn't say who buys them, or where, or when. As if they have always been there, sold with the house. But that isn't how it happened. He must have got them after the divorce, when they sold the apartment, because he claimed it had too many memories for him. But it was mainly because he longed to have a garden.

The bungalow where he now lives with his daughter has a small garden at the back, below the level of the house and surrounded by walls so high they come as a surprise. It feels like being at the bottom of a swimming pool. It hardly ever gets any sunlight, and the sun is a rarity in the region at the best of times. It is a sort of open-air cellar, but still manages to be a delightful spot where two trees, a rowan and an elder, grow facing each other as if in conversation; both bear plentiful parasol-shaped clusters of berries and are meant to bring good luck to lovers. It is always cool there, in a part of the world where no one seeks out cool corners. Jerome has furnished it with an iron table and two chairs that he painted very pale pink on a whim. The result is quite miraculous. It is so beautiful that Jerome never actually sits there, as if it didn't belong to him, as if this ravishing little living room bathed in green shadows was waiting for someone else, not him.

At the end of the summer, when he came home from a week's holiday with Marina, he noticed – over in the bottom right-hand corner, by the water meter – a square flower bed that was not there when they left. Zinnias in every colour, their petals made of velvety scales, wayward dahlias with their great Medusa-like heads, and a few dwarf carnations exhaling a fragrance of cut grass, old roses and vinegar. Marina came and stood beside him.

'Armand's come and planted a bouquet for me. You're not angry, are you?' she asked, taking his arm. 'He wants to be a landscape gardener.'

Jerome thought: If he wants to be a landscape gardener, he'd do well to stop and think for a minute. You don't plant a flower bed bang in front of a door.

The bed ran along the north wall through which the previous owners had knocked a tiny doorway onto the narrow street. Jerome didn't say anything, but Marina added:

'Anyway, we never use that door. You have to bend over double and there's nothing the other side; with this here, if burglars come this way, they'll leave their footprints in the mud and they could easily be traced.'

He nodded in agreement, touched by how perky and vigorous the flowers looked, and by the trouble Armand must have gone to transplanting them, because they were flourishing and in full bloom, as if they had always grown there.

All the same, the damp proved no better for them than the shade. Ten days later, they were bowing their heads. The expression 'bad omen' crossed Jerome's mind.

Now the muddle of brown stems is sprawling on the ground, and the shrivelled, blackened heads with their slimy petals are in the final stages of putrefaction in front of the little doorway. This does nothing to alter the garden's charm, as it welcomes the autumn and its succession of vegetal deaths with equanimity.

The inside of the house is neutral. At least that is what Jerome thought until today. But when he opens his bedroom door, he suddenly sees things as they are: beneath outward appearances of inoffensive banality, every item of furniture is monstrous, poorly designed, and out of place. This is the first time Paula has come to visit him, and it is through her eyes that he is scrutinising his home. It is seven thirty, too late to remedy this painful situation.

He might have time to slap on a coat of paint – he has several cans left in the loft. What's the point, white on white? He realises he is condemned to welcoming his ex-wife into this soulless house.

The kitchen is worst of all with its two battered saucepans, its brown glass mugs and its Pyrex plates with their pet animal designs. 'Do you want your steak on the bulldog plate or the one with the parrot?' Back when he bought them, he must have thought Marina would like the idea. Mind you, she was already thirteen or fourteen, no longer a little girl who leapt for joy at the sight of even the smallest animal.

Anyway, what difference does it make? This isn't about seducing Paula or convincing her of anything. She is coming to bury her daughter's first love. She never met Armand, but tomorrow she will watch his coffin being lowered into the ground.

For the first time in his life, Jerome feels fractionally superior to his daughter's mother. As if he is one up on her. He *did* know the young man with the devastating eyes, the gleaming teeth, the sun-kissed cheeks, the firm, slender neck, the agile body, the vigorous mop of hair, the delicate hands and luminous smile.

Having succumbed to this posthumous inventory, Jerome feels constrained to remind himself that all these wonders have been reduced to nothing, not even ashes. What will they put into the coffin that Paula sees being lowered into the ground? Jerome doesn't know the procedure in cases like this. It's the same with victims of plane crashes or people in natural disasters whose bodies are never found. You do have to put something in the hole. So a coffin, yes, that's the easy bit, but what goes inside it? Nothing? Personal belongings? A photo? Schoolbooks? Recently worn clothes? Who could he ask about this? Jerome can't think. It would be easiest to ask the people at the funeral parlour, but how would he dare?

It is dark now. The girls are still in the bedroom, smoking and talking. Jerome wonders whether he should make them some supper. Are you hungry when you're grieving? He doesn't think so. In films, the pained hero pushes away the plate he is offered. Jerome can see the sequence perfectly. What he has more trouble seeing is how he can be so ignorant. Has he never felt grief? At fifty-six, it seems impossible.

Jerome exerts himself a bit, trawls through his memory and promptly unearths the obvious: his parents dying. Now that, he thinks, was sad. Gabriel felled by cancer and, a few months later, Annette carried off by pneumonia. He was only just twenty. He tries to bring the emotion back to the surface, but feels as if he has too little information available. As if the events had affected someone else, someone close to him, a friend who told him about them. The scenes he can summon up are like something from a TV drama: Gabriel in his hospital bed; Annette throwing a handful of soil onto her husband's coffin; the same Annette on a drip in intensive care; a graveyard in summer, the same graveyard in winter; the solicitor's office.

Strangely, the solicitor's face and voice are still very vivid: long eagle-like nose with dilated pores, tiny eyes tucked deep beneath jutting eyebrows, heavy jowls and a fearsome jaw, a bass baritone that reverberated with a thick south-west accent.

'What does this mean, then, "the found child"?' Mr Coche asks, as Jerome remembers it.

He shrugs his shoulders. Is that how he is referred to in the will?

'A found child?' Mr Coche repeats insistently. 'Hidden children, yes, we've all heard of them. In the war the Jews had to hide their children. Plenty of 'em in my village. All became Catholics. But a found child, what's that, then?'

Jerome sits down on the sofa-bed and rests his chin in his hands. He has always thought of himself as that: a found child.

'In those days,' Annette used to say, 'there wasn't as much

fuss as there is now. Of course, we ended up adopting you, to have papers, and for your inheritance…'

Every time she uttered that word she would open her eyes wide and bat her eyelids, and then burst out laughing.

'Some inheritance! But that's what you are to us, our foundling, our little woodland darling.'

She would stroke his head with her big fleshy hand that gave off a persistent smell of garlic. 'Our little woodland darling,' she would say again, then heave a great sigh, an incomprehensible sigh because it always had a hint of sadness in it.

Jerome knows the story, Gabriel and Annette told it to him whenever he asked, and even when he didn't ask, as if it were a lesson that needed revising, a part to be learnt, as if it were a lie.

It was summertime, Gabriel and Annette had gone for a walk in the woods, under the cool shade of the trees, with all the birds singing (the comment about the birds was from Annette, who thought this detail should not be neglected, that it was a sign). They were walking hand in hand, even though they were hardly in the first flush of youth; they had met a year earlier and were very much in love. 'A pair of lovebirds!' Annette clarified with a note of arrogance.

She had heard twigs snapping behind them, but hadn't turned round, thinking a squirrel or a fawn was following them, and not wanting to startle it.

'I remember the light so clearly,' she added. 'Dappled sunlight everywhere, peeping through the green leaves, like in a fairy tale. Then, when we were just coming out of the woods, the sound of twigs grew louder, but I didn't turn round. I thought it was probably a young boar scampering away behind us. Now, your father's always been hard of hearing, mustn't hold it against him. I didn't turn round, but my heart started beating terribly hard. Maybe I was frightened. Maybe in my imagination the animal had turned into a fully grown boar and was going to mow us down and trample on us. I don't know. I could hardly breathe, but I didn't turn round and I didn't say anything to Gabriel. And then, the exact moment we stepped out of the woods, I felt a little hand in mine. In my left hand I was holding your father's hand, and in my right, the hand of my little woodland darling.'

At this point, she gave a pause. As he grew up, Jerome gave this silence a name, only for himself, not something he ever said out loud: commemoration.

'You were so filthy and so beautiful. You still are beautiful, but you can't imagine how gorgeous you were then, when you were three. Photos don't put it across. Your eyes were green, and so big, as if they'd swallowed the whole forest, and your chin, it was tilted upwards, so proud, so stubborn. I stopped walking. I almost fainted, but I held out, so as not to frighten you. Your father was so surprised, he hadn't heard anything coming. But the moment he saw you, he knelt down before you and he said... – do you remember what you said, Gabriel? – he said, 'Well, what are you doing here, little man?' and I don't know why, but it made me cry.'

The police were informed. Their searches produced nothing. Officials at the *mairie*, the police station, everywhere, proved utterly cooperative. In 1956 the war was still fresh in people's memories, the need for reparation won the day. 'Wild child chooses himself parents', it was just the sort of story the papers wanted to be printing on the front page. All the same, Gabriel and Annette abstained from generating any publicity whatsoever about the event. They moved house shortly after the adoption, working their way up from the south to the north-west, erasing their steps as they went, not that anyone was following them. They described themselves as bohemian, and that was also the word used by the few friends who occasionally appeared from the past to come and see them. Jerome had no idea what it meant. He had read in a book of fairy tales about a princess who had a vase of Bohemian crystal, and had deduced from this that his parents were fragile, which he didn't find very reassuring. Sometimes Gabriel would go away for two or three weeks, 'for his work', Annette used to say. But at other times she would be the one who went away and, when she did, Gabriel gave no explanation.

'Annette's not here, is she?'

'No.'

'When's she coming back?'

'Soon.'

And, as his father didn't seem worried, neither was Jerome.

Annette and Gabriel were different from other parents, the ones Jerome saw at prize-givings or football matches. They were much older and never talked about mundane things like coughs and colds, the weather and good or bad teachers. They didn't invite anyone to the house, but the place never felt gloomy. There was always music and talking. Jerome didn't understand how his parents could have so much to say to each other. They occasionally had violent rows. Things were smashed against walls. They insulted each other in a strange gobbledegook that made their voices sound different. Eventually a door would slam, and calm would be restored immediately. Huddled in his bedroom, Jerome would keep repeating the words 'little woodland darling' as if creating a crown for himself, a helmet that would block out all other sounds.

Now he wonders what on earth he could have been up to in those apocryphal woods before he found Annette's hand to hang on to. He doesn't know how long he spent there. Whether he survived by gnawing on roots, whether a she-wolf suckled him. As a teenager he asked his parents about it, and they replied: 'We don't know everything. And even when we think we do know everything, we're usually wrong. You'll just have to picture yourself as a Mowgli or a Tarzan. Beware people who have a pedigree.' Needless to say, Jerome didn't know what his parents meant by that. To him, pedigree was a word used at dog shows. He couldn't see the connection.

Lying on Paula's bed, he thinks of all the things he only understood too late, and of everything that he will never know. Treacherous words, such as 'bohemian' and 'pedigree', stories that have no beginning or end, like his own or Armand's.

It is in this state that he falls asleep, having failed to give the girls anything to eat, or to have eaten himself, because he is grieving.

2

Paula knocks on the door. No one opens it. She rings the bell. No reaction. She thumps with her foot, her handbag, she calls and shouts. It's a freezing cold night. The taxi took a long time to find the house because of the fog. Not a single light on in this back-of-beyond place. Eleven thirty and everything's dead already. What a dump. She should have gone to a hotel in Besançon. She knocks, hammers and shouts again. What a prick, what a bloody prick, she thinks. He must be in a lovely deep sleep with earplugs in. That's him all over, that is. The man who never hears anything. The man who never moves. Can't believe I still resent him. Time passes, but nothing changes. My anger's still intact.

Jerome wakes with a start. He can hear someone knocking on the door, looks at his watch; it is twenty to midnight. He fell asleep and forgot to unlock the door as promised. Go and open up quickly. But rinse out his mouth first? No. Go and open up straight away. He hurries into the corridor and narrowly avoids slipping on the rug in the hall by saving himself on the door handle, which gives way beneath his weight.

There's no one on the doorstep. The road deserted. He dreamt it.

Paula arrives quarter of an hour later. She gives the tiniest ring of the bell, afraid of waking her daughter. She feels ridiculous with her suitcase. She should have brought a holdall, but everything happened so quickly.

Jerome opens the door immediately.

She's so old, he thinks.

He's so good-looking, she thinks.

They give each other a heartbreaking little kiss hello, and Jerome invites his ex-wife in.

'Come in, we'll put your things in the living room. I've made up the sofa-bed. I don't know if it's comfortable. I've never slept on it.'

Paula looks around, curious and suddenly excited by this escapade.

'I like your house,' she says.

Jerome is so surprised by this comment that he gives Paula a long, probing stare. He studies her and the net result is: he sees her. Not all that old, actually. Not at all old, even, he thinks, looking at her bust, which is still very high, as if her breasts were smiling. She is wearing jeans that could be Marina's and her hair is both short and long, glossy, nicely arranged around her head, like a child's bonnet.

'How do you think I look?' she asks, looking away.

Jerome was not expecting that. Not a question like that, or the mixture of emotions bombarding him. He was expecting reproach, fresh resentment.

'Don't worry about it,' she swiftly corrects herself. 'I don't know what's come over me. I've lost track of things with this whole business. It feels so wrong. Do you think Marina's sleeping? I've got to see her. It'll get my head straight. During the flight there were times when I felt like she was the one who'd been killed. I practically found out this boy existed in the same sentence as I found out he was dead.'

'Didn't she ever talk to you about him?'

Paula shakes her head.

Once again, Jerome can't help savouring a sense of adulterated pride. How can he have such misplaced self-importance?

'He was such a nice boy,' says Jerome. 'Very attractive.'

Paula opens her eyes wide, lost for words. Jerome thinks for a moment and carries on.

'Yes, attractive. Because of his skin. And he had a very wide, very happy smile. I didn't see much of him. He and Marina were always out, but every time we met, I felt... How can I put this? You're going to laugh at me. I felt a sort of lump in my heart.'

'A lump in your heart?' Paula reiterates before roaring with laughter.

Then she smacks her hand over her mouth.

'I'm ashamed of myself. Ashamed of myself. How horrible. Why am I laughing like that? Look, this is your fault too. You're so odd. You've changed. Are you seeing someone?'

'How do you mean?'

'Have you got someone in your life? A woman? A man, maybe?'

Paula laughs again, bites her lip, puts her head in her hands.

'I've got to calm down.'

'Do you want to see Marina?'

Paula looks up, looks at Jerome for a long time.

'No. Not now, not right away.'

'Are you afraid?'

Jerome takes Paula to the bedroom. After knocking and hearing no answer, they open the door. The girls are in the double bed, sleeping at right angles to each other. Marina's head is resting on Rosy's stomach.

'Don't wake her,' Paula whispers.

They close the door again, as they had dozens of times in the past when Rosy slept over at the house, when there was school the next morning, and when they had to tell the girls to stop giggling and talking every five minutes. The girls would laugh all the louder, hiding under the blankets. Then, on the tenth visit, they would find them asleep, sometimes in each other's arms, sometimes head to tail or, like this evening, in a T shape, one girl's ear on the other's stomach.

'Time passes, but nothing changes,' Paula says, back in the living room.

Hearing these words, Jerome knocks his shin on the sofa. It's what she said in his dream. But there's nothing odd about that, really – it's a typical pronouncement for Paula, who has always had a taste for paradox.

'Do you want something to eat?' he asks, rubbing his leg.

Paula smiles, her eyes shining.

Still just as greedy, thinks Jerome, gripped with sudden desire for his ex-wife's forbidden body. His hands are shaking again, like when he was reading the account of the accident. They shake as he opens the tin of sardines, puts a square of butter on a saucer, uncorks the wine. He feels hot all over. Images that he tries to drive away are piling into his head. Armand and Marina in each other's arms, kissing, naked. It's unbearable, terribly uncomfortable. He furrows his brow, as if a frown could dispel the vision. But he succeeds only in modifying it and seeing Paula in Armand's arms. Paula, but much smaller, with her head on the young man's chest. Armand's olive skin, Paula's fair freckled skin.

'Give me your jacket, it's hot,' he says, taking it from her.

She is wearing a short-sleeved T-shirt, and, seeing the skin of her arms, mother of pearl dotted with oat bran, Jerome wants to bite it, to grasp her bicep like a chicken joint and sink his teeth into it. Instead, he folds Paula's jacket in two, then four, then eight, as if planning to fit it in a handbag. She watches him do it, smiles again, takes his hand, moves closer, presses her body against his and wraps her arms round his neck.

He wants to reciprocate the hug, but is overcome by the touch of her skin.

'It's so sad,' he wails with a sob, his body shuddering as he cries. Despite his efforts to control himself, he howls, his mouth twisted, and carries on mumbling, 'We're going to miss him so much.'

His crying grows louder. Paula pulls away from him. She has never seen him in such a state. When she left him, she was afraid he would fall apart, but he held up remarkably well. 'I understand your reasons,' he would say, when she hadn't given him the least explanation, and even though he never understood anything, which was precisely why she had left. Because nothing ever got to him. As if he had no feelings.

She feels devastated and jealous. What was wrong with her that she couldn't produce such colossal pain in him? And if she had been the one to die, would he be so tormented? She knows he wouldn't.

'Do you have any bread?' she asks, sitting at the kitchen table.

Jerome blows his nose, splashes his face with water.

'Sorry,' he says, handing her half a baguette. 'I don't know what's wrong with me. I feel... I don't know.'

'Sit down and eat,' says Paula. 'And drink too. Let's both drink. Let's get a bit drunk.'

Jerome sits down and takes a taste of sardine on a piece of buttered bread from the end of the fork that Paula offers him. He has never eaten anything so good.

She watches him, scrutinises him, studies him.

'What have you been up to for four years?'

Jerome smiles, sniffs. His tears have ebbed completely, he feels light-headed, almost playful. I'm going mad, he thinks, and, because he hasn't answered, Paula asks the question again:

'What have you been up to for four years? Don't you want to tell me?'

They clink glasses, then drain them.

'I've sold houses,' he eventually replies.

'Apart from that, apart from selling houses?'

'Apartments. I've also sold apartments... and building plots too!' he adds, clinking his glass against hers again.

Paula savours her sardines. She likes eating so much that watching her can raise an appetite. In her mouth, the tinned fish seems to melt like the finest flesh.

'Haven't you had enough of that job?'

'No, why? I get about. I meet people.'

'You couldn't give a stuff about people.'

'Really?'

'Well, you don't give a stuff, do you?'

Jerome thinks for a moment. He can't think of anything to contradict this. Not a single counter example.

'Yes, you're right, I couldn't give a stuff,' he admits.

A weight lifts from his chest as he says it.

'Well, that's really nice,' says Paula bitterly.

'But you said it.'

'Maybe I said it to hear you say it wasn't true.'

Jerome recognises Paula's tactics, this encircling strategy that she used against him so many times: start by making the enemy feel confident, butter him up, make him think you're on his side, then all of a sudden, U-turn, attack, immobilisation.

'With Armand it's different,' he murmurs.

'What the hell did he do to you? Did you fall in love or something? I wouldn't be at all surprised to see you batting for the other side. You've always been odd. Odd with women, odd about sex. What have you been up to for four years? I've been with seven men: I slept with five and just had one kiss with two, but I still count them.'

Jerome feels a hefty pain driving into his side, just beneath his heart. A long dagger probing into his left lung. He wants to get out of the kitchen, leave the house, go down into the garden, crawl along the wilting flower bed, slither through the little doorway, set off down the alley, then onto the flight of steps behind the houses, to walk out in the cold, damp night with its seeping smell of trees, take the rutted road that leads to the woods, and run through the dead leaves, getting tangled in brambles, tripping over logs, sprawling with his nose in a puddle, digging beneath the leaves, between the roots, in the mud, making a burrow for himself where he can breathe in his own breath and feel instantly at rest, falling asleep, there, in the woods, in the earth, beneath the leaves.

When he was young, Jerome didn't want to be an estate agent. At school he was entitled to an interview with the careers advisor. She asked him to describe his hobbies, what he liked, what he was passionate about. He sat mutely for a long time, looking at his muddy trainers and the filthy hem of his trousers.

'What do you do in your free time, at the weekends?' Madame Guillermet said, to encourage him. Jerome could tell he shouldn't admit the truth, shouldn't confide in her that he walked through the forest for hours on end, looking for a clearing, a patch of perfectly peaceful undergrowth steeped in velvet light and a cathedral silence broken only by the soft, incomprehensible words of the birds. He sometimes lay down on a bed of foliage, rolling in the twigs, digging at the earth with the tips of his fingers, tentatively at first, but eventually going berserk and scratching at it like a truffle pig, sniffing at the smell trapped under his fingernails.

Building dens, he thought to himself. That might do: I like

building dens out of wood. But he was getting a bit old for that. So, in order to stop the increasingly impatient Madame Guillermet from drumming on the wood of the desk that separated them, he announced in as firm a voice as he could muster, but without looking up at her:

'Building. I'd like to build houses.'

'An architect, then?' she proceeded with a sigh of relief. 'You could become an architect. Let's have a bit of a look at your grades.'

After studying his file with a horrified expression, she announced in a clipped voice:

'You're making a fool of me. Have you seen your marks? Do you think you can become an architect with averages like that? You're pretty lucky you haven't been asked to leave school already. But an architect? No way, no way, don't even think it. Thirty-five per cent for French, twenty for maths... You're going to have to lower your sights, my young friend. Let's have a look... You like houses? Well, you can be an estate agent, then, can't you. No need for qualifications, no need to read, hardly need to count.'

Jerome then remembered that the estate agents' firm in the small town he cycled to every day to get to school was called GUILLERMET ESTATE AGENTS. It had a large white shop front, opposite the church, and its window was always lit up with neon, even in bright sunlight. Monsieur Guillermet sat there reading his paper, with his feet up on his desk. Perhaps he thought about his wife, the careers advisor, who, in the evenings, after supper, took pleasure in calling him a lazy slob, a good-for-nothing, a loser.

'Several women…' he starts to say, breaking the silence. 'Several women…'

But he can't see how to finish the sentence.

'Have you been in relationships? Or was it just a fuck every now and then for survival?'

Jerome is embarrassed, he feels he has never had such an intimate conversation with Paula. It feels vulgar. He imagines this is how men talk amongst themselves when they are all mates together.

All mates together, what a mystery that is. Yet another.

'I remember there were quite a few hovering around you,' Paula goes on, noticing that he is refusing to confide in her. 'The primary school teacher, what was her name again, the one who always wore boots, even in summer? You know who I mean, with teeth like a horse? And there was Miss Tornado 2000, the woman who sold vacuum cleaners. You can't have forgotten her!'

'She sells washing machines now,' he comments absently.

'Pretty exciting stuff, hey, social advancement through electrical appliances. Is that all you can think of to say?'

Jerome takes a deep breath and blurts:

'Several women were hovering around, like you said, but…
I couldn't, I didn't see how… So anyway.'

'Impossible,' Paula declares instantly. 'Impossible. You're
lying. No one's like that.'

Jerome shrugs.

'But you must have urges, dreams, longings? It must eat you
up *sometimes* – how do you cope?' asks Paula.

Jerome realises that 'I go for walks in the woods' still isn't a
satisfactory answer. It is the truth, though. He goes for walks in
the woods. Occasionally he comes across a black grouse, a
badger or a fox. Animals don't run away from him. They stop,
come over, sniff at him. If he is absolutely sure he won't meet
anyone, he goes down on all fours beside them, growling very
softly. It never lasts long. He doesn't want to take any risks. He
knows that if anyone caught him, it would be the death of him.
He never thinks about these walks, doesn't premeditate them,
and barely remembers them. It is something he does,
something he always has done, but it shouldn't happen and no
one must know about it.

He and Paula eat and drink in silence. Time passes, but
nothing changes, thinks Jerome. Four years of not seeing
Paula, and suddenly they're eating together, as if nothing
had happened. How could he bear being away from her? He
wants to tell her he's missed her, but it isn't true. He never
thinks about his ex-wife, apart from when he looks at

weather maps, the perfect disc of the sun hanging like an immutable halo over the south. And even then it isn't her he thinks about. It's a purely climatological daydream, devoid of emotion.

For all these years, there was his work, the grade sheets that Marina brought home like stained clothes that could never be cleaned, and her friends pitching up at the house, their music, their games. The constant to-ing and fro-ing of teenagers, their dates, their laughter, their overly loud voices, full of excitement, projected like stage actors, for an imaginary audience. Their infatuations and their loathings. At times, his daughter would leave him, for a week, a fortnight, a month. She would go to stay with her mother. This brutal recurring void always caught him out. Yoghurts sat in the fridge beyond their use-by date. He left the radio on from morning till night, even when he went to work. He was fascinated by scientific programmes, he made notes that he then archived in a cardboard box. He never re-read them, sometimes wondered whether economics was a science and whether his material about the GDP of developing countries or the impact of the housing crisis on investments in the stock exchange deserved to live alongside his files on superconductive materials, types of functional aphasia and octopuses' brains. Learning, he discovered one evening from a debate dedicated to the work of Isaak Babel, was, according to that writer, the best remedy for depression. Was he depressed? Was he really learning anything from listening to strangers outlining their work?

'The funeral's at ten o'clock,' says Jerome, clearing the table.

'Did you know his parents?'

'No. They're Italian originally, I think. I've never even seen them.'

'I wonder what sort of state they're in.'

'I don't know. Losing a child…'

'Losing a child,' Paula repeats.

'It's like you're not completely alive, after something like that. Don't you think? It's like an illness. I always think that if it happened to me, I'd be ashamed.'

'Ashamed?'

'Yes. I'd feel like I couldn't be with other people any more. As if I had leprosy. Or maybe it's the exact opposite. I'd be really superior. I'd have experienced the worst possible suffering. After that, people who came and whinged about a cold, a tax adjustment or an infidelity, well, I'd feel like killing them. Actually, I think I'd feel like killing everyone.'

'Me too,' says Paula, starting on a second bottle. 'I'd be angry too. But I wouldn't feel ashamed… Actually, yes, you're right. I'd be ashamed of being alive still. In fact, I think I'm the person I'd most want to kill.'

35

'No way of knowing, is there?'

'I don't want to know. I wish this whole business didn't exist in the first place.'

'How do you make something not exist?'

'By not believing in it.'

'But we have to believe in it. The funeral's tomorrow.'

'What if we didn't believe in it just for tonight?'

'We'll have to finish this bottle.'

'Well, let's drink, then,' says Paula, filling their glasses.

'To your love life,' offers Jerome, raising his glass.

'To love in general,' Paula corrects him. 'Let's be generous. Let's raise the stakes. What is love, anyway?'

It's Marina and Armand. Armand and Marina, thinks Jerome, but he doesn't say so.

'It's when you smile if you think about the other person. When you're so desperate to say their name that you're prepared to talk complete nonsense just to say it, to hear it,' he declares.

'The first time I saw you,' Paula starts, her diction beginning to be subtly altered by the wine, 'I thought you looked like Clint Eastwood. When I talked to my friends about you, I called you Clint.'

'Well then, that's because you were in love with Clint Eastwood,' Jerome suggests. 'Otherwise, you'd have said Jerome.'

Paula is struck by his implacable reasoning.

'So I never loved you?'

'No. You loved an American actor and I was a passable double for him.'

'What about me, whose double am I?'

'Shirley MacLaine's!' Jerome announces, amazing himself with this revelation. He has never thought of it before.

Paula flaps her hands. They laugh. Drink. Laugh again. Jerome is struck by the image of them as two old demons dancing on an angel's grave. All the cruelty, the triumph, the horror of years flown by, the jealousy and the sense of injustice. 'Give us back our youth,' plead the greying devils. 'We're old enough now to know what to do with it.' Then the image vanishes. It slinks off to join their sadness, lost in some corner of the night. All that remain are their intoxication, the warmth of their bodies, the night kitchen and the clandestine meal.

After that, not knowing what to do next, they make love. It happens on the living-room sofa. In a mood of terror that the girls might wake, a mood of indecency, and an alcoholic haze. It happens in the past. They don't know how they got undressed, don't look at each other's moonlit bodies. Their eyes are closed, they know the way. The letter S in Braille, then the E, then the X. Every gesture wakes a hundred others, a thousand, until the very first is rediscovered, in all its clumsiness and enthusiasm. They are fifty years old, then forty, thirty-five, thirty, twenty-six, twenty-one. They have just met. They have been walking hand in hand for an hour, hoping that all that ground covered will exhaust them, soothe their hearts, and take this unbearable weight, this frantic need, from them. They want to believe that the distance travelled is making their legs feel wobbly and accelerating their pulse rates, when it is the exact opposite. It is the distance still to be covered that torments and weakens them. They don't have a single muscle left, a single tendon, they are drained, breathless, empty-headed. But where to go? Jerome shares a room with a maths student who revises day and night. Paula lives with an aunt who is bedridden following a cycling accident. The whole town is closed, not one alcove or sheltered spot, spying passers-by everywhere, doors opening, gawpers leaning from windows. The lovers don't speak, they are serious, threatened, on a mission, plagued by desire. So, on they walk, tragic and long-suffering as exiles. The darkness thickens around them, the town starts to fray, the black dome of the hillside draws nearer. They run. The houses are spaced further apart now, fields open up. They run faster. Paula wants to stop, right here, in a ditch, and do it straight away, very quickly, and be done with this cumbersome joy. But Jerome pulls her along behind him, speeds up again, sees trees looming beyond the hedges. They cross a stream and the water seeps into their shoes, freezing.

One more step and they dive into the woods. They don't have enough hands for all that unbuttoning, tearing off and undoing, not enough mouths, not enough of anything. They scatter themselves, don't understand, crawl over each other and draw apart, their heads resting on opened husks, their backs on a carpet of chestnuts.

3

In the morning, the scene is familiar. Breakfast table, mummy, daddy, child. But everything is messed up. Someone has given the stage set a good kick. The child is sitting on the mother's lap, but she's not a baby any more, she's a young woman. She *is* crying like a baby, but it will take more than a bottle to calm her down. Over her head, the mother is biting into bread and jam with an expression that is either cold or mischievous, hard to tell. The father is watching them, dazed.

'I'd better go,' says Rosy, who has stayed outside the tableau. 'I'll try to catch the first hour of lessons because we've got a test on Friday. I'll photocopy everything for you,' she adds to Marina. 'Afterwards we're all planning to meet at the football pitch to go…'

Rosy doesn't finish her sentence. She refuses to say the word 'funeral', the word 'cemetery'; no question of making a concession like that to death. She blows a kiss and leaves the house.

Jerome would have preferred her to stay, but Rosy is intransigent. Mustn't let anything go, Jerome repeats to himself. She's right. Mustn't let anything go. But it's already a lost cause. Unlike the teenage girl, he has no idea what he is supposed to be holding on to. He can tell he should be saying something, making some decisive utterance, bringing an end to this absurd breakfast.

'Will you help me choose something to wear?' Marina asks her mother in a clear voice.

'Of course, my baby,' Paula says, stroking her child's head.

She doesn't look at Jerome. She has not looked at him once since they got up. As if he didn't exist. He is obviously going to have to forget last night, it will have to be found a place in the file marked unexplained, ineffable, forgotten.

Strictly no remembering, Jerome chants, as if reading a sign on the kitchen wall, and all at once, he has no idea why, he feels the relief of someone who has come up with a slogan for themselves. Strictly no remembering anything hurtful or awkward. Because if you remember it, you think about it, you talk about it, you ask yourself questions and it comes back and prowls, like a ghost.

But wily bodies hold on to the memories you want to rid them of. In the dark, Jerome's hands knew where they belonged under Paula's buttocks and Paula's buttocks greeted them as softly as ever. Jerome's feet remembered everything about Paula's ankles. Their skin held no trace of reproach.

This is a day for grieving, Jerome thinks, trying to be sensible. But, in spite of everything, some part of him continues to rebel. The word 'poppycock' clamours inside his head. Why is grief more important than anything else? Jerome revolts against the idea. Then he thinks of Armand and the pain of his death, and sees clearly that it is more powerful, more tangible, more fixed and more certain than everything else around him. Take a tree in your arms and pull upwards, try to lift it up. You see, nothing moves, and that's what death is like, thinks Jerome.

They are the first at the cemetery. Marina clings to the metal gate and rests her head on its bars. An icy cold has dropped down suddenly from the cloudless sky.

'How can you bear this?' Paula murmurs in Jerome's ear. 'When it's this cold in October?'

Good of her to make conversation, he thinks, because what is really unbearable at the moment is neither the temperature nor the arctic swirl of the wind, any more than the blinding sunlight bouncing off stone structures; it is their child imprisoned in her own distress, her reddened hands gripping metal. It is the rug that has been pulled from under their feet, turning life's chronology upside down. The first time a young woman goes to a cemetery, it is to bury a grandparent, an old aunt, her father or her mother.

Jerome replies that it is a very hearty sort of cold, but his words are masked by the rumbling of the hearse labouring unwillingly up the hillside.

Marina turns round, her eyes wide, horrified that the car is here. Jerome looks up at the sky so as not to meet his daughter's eye. Paula rushes to catch her child's body as it collapses.

We'll never cope, he thinks to himself as he kneels stroking the unconscious Marina's face. If only she could stay like this, sleeping in her parents' arms and waking only later, much later, after the earth has filled in the grave, after the grass has grown over it, after she has found a new love, after the birth of her children. After.

The coffin is displayed before the grave. In a matter of minutes a forest of people has formed around it. They came on foot, by car, by moped, by bicycle. Their numbers keep on growing. The whole village is here.

The father and mother and their four remaining sons stand facing the crowd. The boys – tall, burly lads with impossibly long eyelashes and bruise-coloured lips – look furious. The mother is glancing to one side as if waiting for something or someone. The father stands slightly apart, a huge man, with the bulk of a rustic wardrobe in his thick overcoat. He doesn't blink, doesn't breathe. A bird, mistaking him for an oak tree, has landed on his shoulder. No one seems to have noticed. Jerome wants to draw someone's attention to this apparition, he feels it would lighten the atmosphere, but knows it would be inappropriate; it's even inappropriate to think about it. Yet that, and that alone, is what he is thinking about, wondering whether it's a bullfinch, a linnet or just a robin. Is that you, Armand? a tiny voice inside his head asks.

The gaggle of teenagers are standing, holding hands, to the right of the coffin. They are all crying, in silence, girls and boys alike. Marina is with them. Her legs can't support her. Arms take it in turns, round her back, under her armpits, behind her thighs. Her feet are barely touching the ground. She is levitating.

Mathias, an awkward great lump who stands head and shoulders taller than his friends, and whose Adam's apple keeps bobbing up and down in his long thin neck, has spotted the bird. Jerome is sure of it. Mathias elbows Denis and tilts his chin towards Armand's father. Jerome lip-reads the word 'robin'. A muttering ripples round the teenagers.

Another, more snide, muttering spreads among the villagers. 'Where's the priest? Have you seen the priest?' The funeral directors exchange helpless looks. The hearse driver steps tentatively towards Armand's father and the bird flies away. An 'oh' of disappointment, a sigh sung in unison, goes up and dies away instantly in the freezing air. Armand's father steps aside, and from behind him, as if from a wardrobe, a little old woman appears in a long cape and a black headscarf. This tiny, upright, austere figure goes over to the coffin and lays on it a hand as light and gnarled as an autumn leaf. She shakes her head, mumbling words that no one understands. This is a reprimand, and as she grows more agitated, the onlookers become anxious.

'This isn't how things are usually done,' various people grumble. A sort of grumpiness takes hold. They wanted a sermon, words about paradise to fuel their dreams, about hell to frighten them, about a life picked in the full bloom of youth to make them cry, and about divine justice to offer them relief. Some are already moving away from the cortège and leaving the cemetery. What sort of circus is this? Dry-eyed parents and a grousing witch. A funeral for savages. Never seen anything like it. The old girl hasn't given up. She looks up at the crowd. Stares at them. Tilting her head questioningly. What are you doing here? she seems to be asking. What can you possibly understand about this?

'It's his grandmother,' whispers Zellic, the till operator from the butcher's shop.

The primary school teacher makes her way over to the teenagers. They are all former pupils, from the days when the school had only one class. She kisses them one after the other, holds them in her arms. She retired last year, but still lives in the village. The smack of her kisses breaks the silence.

'Whatever next?' whispers Madame Legrantier, the postmistress. 'Always has to be different, doesn't she?'

Jerome loathes the spiteful comments. He wishes he were more self-assured, could take things in hand. He would remind people they did need to show a minimum level of decency, and that it doesn't really matter what form the ceremony takes, what is important is the mood of reflection and tenderness. He sees himself as a sage, a patriarch.

But the old woman steals his thunder. In a powerful croaky voice, speaking oh so slowly, she pronounces the following words:

'*Una mattina mi son svegliata.*'

The chorus of young brothers joins in, singing very softly:

'*O bella ciao, bella ciao, bella ciao ciao ciao.*'

Then the old woman speaks again:

'*Una mattina mi son svegliata*
Eo ho trovato l'invasor.'

The song grows, becomes more vigorous. Some of the teenagers know the couplet, and join in the refrain. The old woman raises her voice and lifts a clenched fist towards the sky.

At the end of the song, the cemetery is almost empty. The only people left are the parents and brothers, the teenagers, Marina, Jerome, Paula and an elegant gentleman standing some way away, leaning against a tree and apparently drawing in a sketchbook.

'Have you noticed, there aren't any flowers?' Paula whispers in Jerome's ear.

'They're communists,' he replies, as if that explains everything.

Then, before the open grave where the coffin is waiting, Armand's father talks at length. He breaks off from time to time to weep, in no hurry, waits for the sobs to subside and carries on. He says what he has to say in Italian. He probably manages to make a few jokes because, in three places, his sons smile. To conclude, he turns to the teenagers and, in heavily accented French, says:

'When Armand was born, his mama told him: you, my little one, shall never have a Vespa.'

The mother puts her head in her hands, her sons huddle round her.

The father shrugs.

Marina, who has rejoined her parents, agrees:

'I was against it too.'

Jerome hugs his daughter tightly. She rests her head in the crook of his neck and he feels her hot tears trickling over his skin.

'Shall we go?' suggests Paula.

'I'm going to stay with them,' Marina says, pointing towards her friends, who are starting to hop from one foot to the other to battle the cold.

Paula and Jerome watch her dissolve into the crowd of frozen bodies, the spiked hairdos, the shaven heads and others weighed down with shambolic locks.

'That's a good thing,' Paula tells Jerome. 'It's better like that. She needs to be with them. We just don't measure up.'

Jerome recognises the mixture of cowardice and subtle indifference in Paula that has always fascinated him. A casual approach he could never have. *His* thing is stupidity, never thinking of the right thing to say at the right time, slow on the uptake. It is only once they are back in the car that he regrets not saying hello to Armand's parents. But it's too late.

'A leopard can't change his spots,' he sighs as he sets off.

'How do you mean?' asks Paula.

'Marina choosing herself a communist.'

'So? Anyway, it's his family who are communists. Maybe he voted for the Right. Like all those weird youngsters. Those youngsters who vote for the Right.'

'Even so.'

'Even so what?'

'My parents were communists and my daughter falls in love with a communist.'

'You never told me your parents were communists.'

'That's because I never realised.'

Fields spool past on both sides of the car, perfect carpets, shimmering cushions.

'You've gone the wrong way,' Paula says just as they fork right.

'I need to drive for a bit.'

'My train's at one o'clock.'

'Don't you want to leave later? I thought you'd stay... Marina... you didn't say goodbye to her.'

'Oh, you know, at her age, mothers aren't much use any more.'

Mothers, thinks Jerome, are meant to stay at home. They're meant to say: 'I want to see you more often.' They're meant to be there to be rejected.

'Do you think I'm a chauvinist?' he asks.

'Yes. No. I don't know. A couple of minutes ago you were a communist.'

'No, not me. My parents.'

'What's this all about? What's the story?'

'It's the story of my life,' says Jerome, amazed by this burst of lyricism. 'My parents' burial was just like Armand's,' he goes on. 'There were no flowers, no priest.'

'And a witch came out of a thicket and intoned a revolutionary chant?'

'No. There was no grandmother. There was no family, or teenagers. Except for me. Annette was planning to sing an

Aragon song over my father's grave. You know, the one that goes: *It would only have taken one more minute for death to come?*'

'And? Did she not sing it, then?'

'She couldn't do it. Her throat was too tight. She showed me the piece of paper she'd copied the lyrics onto. It was all crumpled. It looked like a rag. I read the poem to myself. I couldn't remember the tune at the time.'

'What about her? What was it like for her?'

'I was on my own. No, I was with Matthieu. Do you remember? My maths-student friend. I'd been planning to sing the song, but I felt ashamed with him there. I kept the piece of paper screwed up in my pocket. I didn't think he'd come. And when I saw him… I was touched and…'

'What did you say?'

'Nothing.'

'Nothing? You didn't say anything?'

'Actually, yes. Matthieu said something. He said: 'You'll never say the word "mum" again.' He was a scientist through and through. It was a logical observation. Except that I'd always called my mother Annette. Still, it did me good to hear that. I don't know why.'

'That's the advantage of mistakes.'

'How do you mean?'

'Mistakes are the best way to get to the truth. You explained that to me. A long time ago.'

'Are you sure you want to go?'

'Yes.'

Jerome negotiates a hairpin bend almost without slowing down. The car swerves. Paula clings to the handle over her door. She is giddy with speed, carried away by this flash of spirit from her ex-husband, yesterday's lover. She puts her hand on his knee, but Jerome flinches away as if burnt by her touch.

'Oh, sorry,' she says.

'Sorry for what?'

'For everything,' she replies with a sob, the first since she arrived. 'For nothing. For this shitty life. Why do we never get on?'

Because you're brutal, thinks Jerome.

'Because I'm one sandwich short of a picnic,' he says. 'I've got a bit missing.'

He so wants her to ask him about this. For her to take the time to wonder which bit he means. For her to rewind all the way back to the luminous woodland labyrinth that saw him being born. He wants her to get the truth out of him, the real truth he doesn't know the first thing about. For her to torture him to get him to confess it.

'It's too late now,' Paula announces.

'Too late for what?'

'To talk to each other. We should have started with that, but we got it wrong. We read the map the wrong way round.'

Jerome parks outside the house. At the top of the steps, leaning against the front door with the same elegance as he had against the tree in the graveyard, is the man with the sketchbook.

'What's that guy doing here?' asks Jerome.

'Who do you mean?'

'The guy at the top of the steps. He was at the funeral.'

'Maybe he's a journalist,' suggests Paula.

They get out of the car and head towards the stranger.

'Hello,' says the man, reaching out to shake Jerome's hand. 'I'm Inspector Cousinet. Could I talk to you?'

Jerome asks the inspector in and offers him a chair in the living room.

'I'll leave you to it,' says Paula. 'I'm going to pack my things. Will you take me to the station? We need to leave in twenty minutes.'

'Don't worry. I won't be long,' says Cousinet.

Jerome sits down opposite the inspector.

'Aren't you going to ask me why I'm here?' the man asks.

Jerome doesn't reply. A grimace barely flickers over his face.

'Have you spoken to a police inspector before?'

'Since the accident?'

'No, since whenever. In your life.'

'No, never. I've spoken to policemen, about speeding fines.'

'That's different.'

'I can imagine. But I thought you were a painter. What's that book?'

'It's my notebook!' Cousinet replies, laughing.

'Do you draw?'

'I draw, I write, I scribble shopping lists. Don't *you* have a notebook?'

'What for?'

'Well, I don't know. Make a note of your thoughts.'

I don't have any thoughts, Jerome comes close to saying. But that's not true. Since Armand's death, he hasn't stopped having them. The exhaustion crushing him for the last few days is just that, it's because of the thoughts. All those abortive hypotheses, lame verdicts and incongruous questions. He's not used to it.

'Would you like to see?' offers the inspector, handing the thing to him.

'No, no!' Jerome cries in spite of himself.

'It's not dangerous, it's not a gun,' says Cousinet, laughing again.

'No, but it's… it's private.'

'Tut tut tut. Mustn't confuse the two. It's not my private diary. It's my notebook.'

'And do you have a private diary?'

'Well, if I told you, that would be getting private. It's a funny question, though, don't you think?'

'You're trying to confuse me. Don't you think I'm confused enough already? What do you want?'

'Ah, there we are. Now we get to it. Congratulations! Have to pull out all the stops to arouse your curiosity.'

That's not true, Jerome wants to reply. I was instantly curious about you because of your clothes, the way you stood and that damn notebook. But he derives a strange feeling of pride from being seen as a tough nut to crack.

'I have concerns of my own,' he pronounces, trying to be enigmatic.

'Good, good. Nothing like a few concerns!' exclaims Cousinet, still just as cheerfully. 'So, in answer to your question, I want to talk to you about Clementine Pezzaro. Or actually no, no. That's going too fast. I want to talk to you about the young.'

'The young in general?'

'Yes, in general. And also in particular. I want to talk to you about young people who disappear.'

Paula pops her head round the door.

'I'm really sorry, but...'

'The train won't wait,' says Cousinet, getting to his feet nimbly. 'I won't keep you any longer. I'll come and see you at work, if you don't mind, Mr Dampierre.'

Jerome sees the inspector to the door and watches him don

a wide-brimmed felt hat which completes his air of sophistication.

'What did he want?' asks Paula from behind Jerome.

'It doesn't matter.'

4

It is a white morning. Opaque sky, frost, loneliness. Estate agents, even on the main square of a small town, see little activity on weekday mornings. Jerome is absent-mindedly perusing a file. What people are looking for on the left, what's on offer on the right. The latter rarely corresponds to the former. In fact they never correspond. You're better off not being too much of a matchmaker if you want to cope with the constant disparity between what people want and what is available.

Who, for example, can he sell this building to, way out in the country, made up of a wooden barn with a covering of corrugated iron, and a piggery with cob walls and a slate roof, all on a one-hectare plot? Jerome contemplates the details and thinks he could perfectly easily be happy there himself.

On the picture he took, he makes out several of his favourite species of tree: a weeping willow, three silver birches, an elm, an ancient pear tree and a profusion of hawthorn along a hedge line. He could go to work by bike. In spring, buttercups would unroll their brilliant carpet under his windows. At night he could watch the stars through a skylight in the roof. He would have a donkey and a goat in an enclosure. No need to connect up to mains water or electricity, he knows where the nearest stream is and has always had a weakness for candlelight. Forty thousand euros. He doesn't have it. What a shame. Meanwhile, Mr and Mrs Rumidet, whose list of requirements is at the top of the other pile, have three hundred thousand euros to spend, which will not be enough to buy the manor house – in a lovely elevated position and requiring no work at all – that they long for.

What an absurd job, he thinks. The matchmaker comes to mind again. For estate agency to work better, you would have to apply the techniques of arranged marriages. The future couple don't like each other and have never met, but, with time, the groom will get used to the wart on his intended's nose; she, in turn, will end up seeing the good side of her betrothed's nastiness; eventually, he will like the hairs that grow on his wife's earlobes, and she won't know how to cope without her husband's sly glances.

How about taking the Rumidets to look at the piggery? he wonders.

People are busying round the village square, by car, on foot, trailing a shopping trolley, manoeuvring a buggy. I know them all, thinks Jerome.

Some of them went to school with him, others sat their driving test at the same time. He remembers the days when the old were the young, when the housewives were little girls. When he meets someone in the street, he says hello, but both parties keep their distance; no question of the past mortgaging the present. We used to walk down the street with a casual arm around each other's shoulders, we couldn't shake hands now. His years at boarding school, a temporary exile to a nearby town, and various job transfers have helped build comfortable cotton-wool walls separating and protecting former classmates, the members of a now-disbanded sports team, companions from shooting expeditions replaced by solitary escapades on a quad bike.

That woman with red hair, almost orange over her temples, with a cigarette hanging from her lip and her bust sagging over her tummy to form a single great lump that her thin legs, tapering into ski boots, can barely carry, that woman who doesn't even turn to look at Jerome, he kissed her when he was thirteen, his hands clamped onto her breasts that were the shape and consistency of mandarin oranges. It was behind the supermarket warehouse. She can't have forgotten. He never thinks about it himself. It's more surreal than a dream. It's completely unrelated to the rest of his life, like some grotesque pointless episode that still leaves a trace; such a tiny trace that the figure has hardly vanished round the corner of the street before he starts doubting the anecdote.

'Good morning, my little man!' exclaims a voice coloured with an accent.

Jerome is startled. A tall woman with short dark hair, a solid frame and wide, smiling face has just come into the office.

'Good morning,' he replies. 'What can I do for you?'

'My little man is going to find me a little house,' she says, sitting down without an invitation.

She wraps one leg round the other, rests her elbows on the desk, wedges her chin between her hands and looks at Jerome, wide-eyed.

A loony, he thinks.

'Are you American?'

'God no! What a thought! American? Do I look like an American?'

'I don't know. I said it because of your accent.'

'You don't know much about accents. I'm Scottish.'

'My apologies.'

'Accepted.'

'Excuse me?'

'I accept your apologies. That's what you say, isn't it?' she asks, bringing her face even closer.

She has huge hazel eyes beneath eyebrows as fine as a baby's, barely interrupting her forehead, which is also enormous. The size of an animal's head, thinks Jerome. Not so much a face as a soup plate. The word 'trophy' also comes to mind, perhaps because of the prominent cheek bones, the narrow, clearly defined lips, the long, very straight nose and the determined chin.

'What are you looking for?'

She slumps heavily against the back of the chair and, in the same movement, drops her knees apart, which draws Jerome's attention to her long thin legs drowned in jeans too big for them.

'Bah, the impossible,' she replies. 'Otherwise it's no fun. I'm looking for a small house, but with some soul, with big old trees, but not too many of them, cow parsley by the door and, if possible, a well with a chain and a pulley that goes eek-eek-eek.'

Jerome is not sure what to put on the form.

'You're the first estate agent I've been to,' she adds. 'I've been living in Paris, but it turns out I don't like it. Too friendly, not anonymous enough. Everyone's so kind there, everyone wants to be your friend. I don't like having lots of friends. I like space. I came here because of a book. *The Flint Year*. Have you read it? It's set in this region. It's like prehistory, cold and silent, no humans and lots of animals. Do you like animals? I'm crazy about them. But I kill them, if I have to.'

And she suddenly stops talking. Jerome has listened to none of it, apart from the last two sentences. 'I'm crazy about them.

But I kill them, if I have to.' He hopes she isn't talking about men. Or actually no, he hopes she *is* talking about men.

'Have you got anything to show me?'

'If you're happy to, we'll start by filling in your form. I need to know your surname and first name.'

'My surname's Smith, like everyone else. My first name's Vilno, like no one else.'

'Vilno Smith,' Jerome says as he writes.

'Shall I give you my date of birth?' she asks coyly.

'That won't be necessary for now.'

'20 April 1960. I love my date of birth. Twenty and sixty and April, it's the best month, isn't it?'

'Your phone number?'

'Don't you want to know my marital status? Married? Any children? Divorced? Widowed?'

Jerome sighs as discreetly as possible. He wonders what he has done to deserve this punishment.

'I have a grown-up son of twenty-three who's just finishing his course at Oxford,' she goes on. 'He thinks of himself as English. But I no longer have a husband…'

Vilno Smith lets this sentence dangle in the air, as if hesitating to tell him the rest. Should she give more details? She decides not. Snaps her knees back together smartly, like an old woman her purse.

Jerome is surprised to find himself regretting this move on

his client's part. He is gripped by a violent feeling of nostalgia relating to this whole knee business. He doesn't know why. He wishes she would open them again. It's not sexual, he tells himself. It's deeper than that.

He then thinks that, if he had a notebook like Inspector Cousinet, he would make a note: 'It's not sexual, it's deeper than that.' He can see how it might progress from there. What could be deeper than sex? Why has sex only ever been superficial for me? He could become an intellectual if this carried on. The idea makes him smile.

'Why are you making that face?' asks Vilno Smith. 'Do you think I'm too demanding? It's true. I'm very demanding. With everything. I don't see why we should have to settle for something if it won't do.'

'Completely agree,' says Jerome.

'That's what they call sales talk, isn't it? You pretend to think the same as me to get me to trust you, then you can sell me whatever you like. Oh, and I forgot to say: I've hardly got any money.'

'That's not a problem,' Jerome says. 'It's not an expensive region and lots of people are trying to sell because of the financial crisis. But maybe you'll think that's sales talk?'

'Actually, I've got nothing against sales talk,' Vilno Smith announces. 'In fact, it's more trustworthy than anything else, when you think about it. And I *am* here to buy, aren't I? So, have you got anything to offer me?'

Jerome shows her the picture of the piggery with the slate roof.

'There isn't a well,' he points out.

'That's a shame, but I like it. The price is very attractive.'

She parts her knees again for a second as she says this, but closes them almost immediately. Jerome forces himself not to look down, to hold her eye.

'We could go there tomorrow, if you'd like,' he suggests.

'Why not today?'

'Today isn't possible,' he says sternly.

He must stand up to her, appear resolute.

'I've got meetings all day,' he adds to stop her insisting.

And tough luck if she doesn't like it, tough luck if it won't do, as she says.

'Tomorrow, then,' she concedes, jumping up. 'Ten o'clock tomorrow.'

'Nine o'clock tomorrow,' he counters.

She wrinkles her nose and turns for the door.

'You haven't given me your phone number,' says Jerome.

'I don't have one,' she replies, not looking back.

The door slams shut.

Jerome watches through the window as Vilno Smith walks away. Her lumberjacket is open, flapping behind her like a cape. She's like a mare, he thinks. Or a heifer. Her words come back to him: 'Do you like animals? I'm crazy about them. But I kill them, if I have to.' She wasn't talking about men, then.

I've got to make an effort, he tells himself. Make an effort to listen and to understand when I'm listening. I must have some neurological problem. I store up information without assimilating it, and it comes back with a time lapse, when it's already too late.

On the station platform a week earlier, Paula said: 'Take care of yourself, big boy.' And then, after a silence: 'Thank you.'

He now realises she was thanking him for that night, love in Braille. But at the time he didn't get it. He thought she was just grateful he had taken her to catch her train. 'It's the least I could do,' he replied. Hardly surprising, then, that he hasn't heard a peep out of her since. He should have thanked her too, let her know that she had brought him back to life, admitted that – thanks to her – his blood that had been frozen for so long had started flowing through his veins once more.

He stands up, closes the office and goes to the newsagent on the other side of the square.

'I'd like a notebook, please,' he says to Sylvie Deshuchères.

'What sort of notebook?' asks the surly newsagent.

Sylvie, he thinks. Little Sylvie, so mature for her age. I remember when you first came to high school. Your satchel was so big, it stuck out in every direction. Like a woman with a sandwich board. Don't act like we've never met. I'm not just the tradesman from the shop opposite; I'm the boy in Year 10 you were in love with. It was for me that you wrote on the wall of the cafeteria at the swimming pool 'our hearts forever', which didn't mean anything.

'A book for making notes,' he clarifies. 'A small notebook you can slip into a pocket.'

The stationer shows him two types, one spiral-bound with squared paper, the other with proper binding and lined paper. Jerome chooses the first, immediately regrets it, but doesn't say so. He pays and walks back across the square. This notebook slipped into the breast pocket of his jacket is an emergency heart, a brain annexe. Armed with this, he feels all-powerful.

He doesn't take off his jacket, but sits at his desk, overcome by a sense of urgency. He grabs a pen, opens the book and writes down the sentence with the animals that should be killed if they have to be, then the one about sex, 'It's not sexual, it's deeper than that.' He expects to carry on, gripped by a furious need to express himself, but he can't remember the ideas that these declarations were meant to lead to. Five minutes ago he was remarkably intelligent, his mind alert, ready to manhandle the most sophisticated concepts, to ask the questions that single-handedly reveal the truth, but here he is now – because of this damned notebook – reduced to stupidity again.

He tries an experiment: he snaps the notebook shut and shoves it in a drawer. After a few seconds, the thoughts start up again. Words whir and stretch and collide with each other. Lots of stuff going on up there, he thinks, pleased with his brain.

Inverse experiment: open the drawer, ditto the notebook. And nothing. Everything dissolves, his mind is as blank as the pages. No echo, no resonance, as if something were broken. He picks the pen up again, brings the tip up to the paper, hopes for a miracle.

Poor Marina, he thinks. She's got her baccalaureate this year. She'll have to write endless exam papers. He doesn't remember writing being this difficult. Poor Marina. Mind you, that's if she goes to the exams. At the moment she's not even going to lessons. She's holed up in her bedroom. Rosy lectures her, brings her food, supplies her with cigarettes. The house is constantly full. In a week, Jerome has got to know his daughter's friends, who, until now, he viewed as so many shadowy figures distinguishable only by their haircuts.

There's Mathias, the blue-eyed stammerer with long hollow cheeks, crowned with a mess of dirty plaits. There's Denis, the short one with glasses who's good at mechanics, revs his engine more than he talks, and shaves his head every Monday. There's heavily made-up Zoe with tiny feet, enormous breasts and shoulders that never stop jigging to some endless internal music. There's Lola, whose nose takes up almost all of her face, a nose like a steamboat, proud but somehow still sinking head first towards her chin. She does very elaborate things with her hair, poking feathers, pencils, twigs and flowers into it as if to divert attention from the fascinating centre of her face. They're all incredibly kind, helpful, polite and gentle. They call Jerome by his first name and he doesn't know why, but he finds it heart-breaking. He wants to thank them for it, to give them some evidence of his gratitude, but doesn't know how to, so he makes them coffee, litres and litres of coffee.

The teenagers are on a constant relay in the corridor, Marina is still invisible. Last Tuesday, Jerome saw her coming out of the bathroom. It was appalling. The loathing he read in her eyes.

Jerome makes a note: 'The loathing in Marina's eyes', and this time the words flow. No effort required. His pen isn't quick enough to follow the tide. 'She wishes I were dead instead of Armand. She wants to be alone and doesn't want me reminding her of her grief. She wants to rewind time and change its course. She wants to be someone else, someone none of this has happened to.' Jerome reads through it. He feels absolutely nothing. The sentences are pointless. They have no impact. He wonders what it is that makes a sentence valid or not.

While he is looking up at the ceiling as if the answer to this thorny question were hanging there, the door to the agency opens.

'Am I disturbing you?' asks Cousinet in a fluty voice, his wide-brimmed hat in his hand.

Jerome feels he has been caught in some compromising act. He can feel the red rising in his cheeks. He hides the notebook under a folder with such violence that the documents inside scatter over the desk and onto the floor, pages borne away by a tornado of shame.

'No, of course not,' he mumbles. 'Not at all. Come in, come in.'

Cousinet sits down, carefully adjusting the crease in his perfectly ironed black trousers.

'I thought it would be easier to meet you at your place of work. I didn't want to disturb you at home. How is your daughter?'

'Not good,' replies Jerome, surprised by the simplicity and candour of this reply.

'Of course,' Cousinet nods, with touching compassion. 'What she's going through is terrible.'

'I don't know what I'd give to...'

Jerome breaks off, his throat constricted.

'You wish she could be spared the pain. You wish you could suffer instead of her, and you can't do anything for her. Times like this are particularly harsh for parents.'

Harsh, Jerome says to himself in silence. Harsh, that's the word. How does he do that, this inspector, find the appropriate word? Say something other than 'tough' or 'difficult'? Did he prepare for this conversation by making notes? Jerome is convinced that Cousinet's notebook is full of expressions as elegant as his clothes, well-cut sentences that drape like fabric cut on the bias.

He nods.

'I'd like to ask you a few questions, if that's all right with you,' says Cousinet.

'I don't know if I'll be able to answer. I don't know anything. Nothing that matters.'

'We think we don't know anything,' says the inspector, 'but most of the time, we're amazed to discover it's the exact opposite. The truth is in the details. In the most insignificant details.'

As he says these words, he takes out his notebook and a fountain pen, a fine, slender silver one. Jerome envies him yet again. He too would like to have a beautiful Waterman.

'Do you remember Clementine?'

Jerome shakes his head. The name doesn't mean anything to him.

'Clementine Pezzaro?' the inspector elaborates.

'No, I don't think so. What's the connection?'

'With Armand? I don't know. Or rather, I don't know yet. Clementine Pezzaro disappeared on 27 August last year. She went to the same school as your daughter. She left home early in the morning and never came back. The police did some research, the local community organised a sort of search. They didn't come up with anything. They dragged the lake, and put her picture up. Don't you remember?'

'I was on holiday. With my daughter. We went away for the last two weeks in August, to a hotel – well, a sort of club – in Sicily.'

Jerome feels himself flushing again. Why did he add that business about the 'club'? He feels ridiculous. He did have to answer, though. You always have to give the police an answer. To be accurate. Not hide anything.

'Perhaps your daughter knew her?'

'I don't know. What happened to her, to this girl?'

'That's what I'm trying to determine. Her father reported her missing the following day. Then he withdrew it. We haven't heard from him since.'

'Well then, he probably found her. Why don't you go and ask him?'

'He's moved away,' replies Cousinet. 'He had a garage, a workshop where he repaired and sold second-hand motorbikes. That's where Armand bought his Triumph.'

A Triumph, thinks Jerome. What a funny name. Armand died triumphantly.

'So you think...' Jerome says hesitantly.

'I don't think anything,' says Cousinet with a smile. 'I'm looking.'

He in turn looks up at the ceiling, as if the answer to this enigma were hanging there too. Questions on the ground, answers in the sky, thinks Jerome, consumed with the urge to take out his notebook and write down this aphorism which has filled him with fleeting cheerfulness.

'I have a theory,' Cousinet goes on after a brief silence. 'Would you be interested?'

Without waiting for Jerome to answer, he proceeds.

'It's a theory about young people. To be precise, about young people who go missing. To be even more precise, about young people who go missing from the country.'

'The rural exodus,' Jerome exclaims stupidly.

Cousinet roars with laughter.

'Yes, yes, it is sort of, if you like. That's an amusing way of looking at it. Not wrong, not wrong at all.'

Jerome is floored by this involuntary flash of humour. Laughing about death, how can that be possible? What sort of punishment could apply to a sin like that?

'I've been doing this job for nearly forty years,' says Cousinet, now serious again. 'I've seen thousands of cases in forty years. I've solved some of them. It doesn't matter much. With time there are sort of themes that emerge. It's also about sensibilities. Some of my colleagues are obsessed with crimes of passion, others with crimes motivated by money, inheritance disputes. It's like with stories, you see. For some people, fairy tales are full of witches, for some it's princesses, and for others it's knights or talking animals. It's the same story for all of them, but depending on who's reading it, the hero changes. In my career, the heroes have always been young people. The ones who die, the ones who disappear, especially in the country. You can't imagine how many of them there are. It's astonishing.'

Jerome promises himself that he will soon use that word: 'astonishing'. He could swear it has never crossed his lips, when he knows what it means and has probably had hundreds of opportunities to say it.

'So what's your theory, then?' he asks.

'Ah, I'm glad I've aroused your curiosity! If you want to know the whole story, I've retired.'

Cousinet stops talking all of a sudden and Jerome has lost track of what is going on. If he's retired, then why is he asking questions? Does he have any right to?

'For a few months now I haven't been making enquiries for money or as a duty. I've been doing it...'

'For the beauty of it?' Jerome asks without thinking.

'Bravo!' exclaims Cousinet. 'That's it! That's exactly it! Jerome – I hope you don't mind if I call you Jerome – you've made my day.'

Jerome feels very hot. He wants to take off his jacket, his shoes even. Embarrassment puts him in a sweat.

'The beauty of it!' Cousinet repeats. 'That's it. The young disappear and, for me, they're like the numbers in a dot-to-dot.

I feel that, if I draw a continuous line from 1 to 300, then from 300 to 1000, and so on, the design will eventually appear. A design which – who knows? – might take the form of a teenager's face!'

Jerome looks down. The inspector notices his discomfort and reins himself in. He can read body language the way others read music or tea leaves.

'I know what you're going through,' he reverts to a more measured tone. 'I'd like to help you. I'm playing the fool to take your mind off it, but it's wrong. Don't go thinking I find these losses, these disappearances, these deaths entertaining. Quite the contrary. I find them excruciating. But what can we do to fight pain other than confront it with understanding?'

Jerome keeps his eyes lowered. He is concentrating so as not to forget that formula: understanding against pain. The equation of my life, he thinks.

'I'll come by again,' says Cousinet. 'I won't disturb you any longer. You've got work to do.'

He stands up and, on the doorstep, offers this parting shot:

'With your daughter, with Marina, think about talking to her. We never talk to the young enough. If she rejects you, it doesn't matter. Talk to her anyway. She's probably waiting for you to show some interest in her. The young are very fragile, very sensitive. They need huge amounts of love and constant attention. They're a bit like bonsais: small on the outside, big on the inside, and vice versa. Being disproportionate like that makes them pretty vulnerable.'

Cousinet closes the door behind him, and Jerome finally looks up to watch him walk away, felt hat on his head, and feline, as if he always walks on tiptoe. He waits until the inspector has disappeared on the far side of the square before taking his notebook out from under the folder.

Nothing comes. It's because of my pen, he thinks.

5

Jerome stops the car just as the sun, which eventually broke through the clouds an hour before it was due to set, disappears, swallowed by the horizon. He parks on a mud track on the edge of the forest and, sitting with his hands resting on his knees, waits for nightfall. He thinks that a perfect death would happen like this, like the end of a day: last rays beaming, shadows in indigo, then grey, a final burst of colour, paler tones persisting in the dark... pause... the first stars appearing.

But death isn't like that. It usually strikes suddenly, out of nowhere, preposterous. Is there still such a thing as a natural death? The news is crammed with catastrophes and accidents. What was it like in the old days? Jerome has no idea. He often regrets that his musings are not matched by knowledge. If he were a doctor, a historian or a sociologist, perhaps he would understand better. He feels his fascination with alternating day and night has always played tricks on him. Some people see the truth in numbers, but ever since he was a child, he has looked for it in dawn and dusk, as if this double switching constituted the definitive metaphor. Appearing in life, disappearing from life, light, darkness. Jerome never abandons duality. He is a victim of the reassuring illusion that it always comes back to the same thing. After night, day, after day, night, and so on, endlessly, on a loop. Based on this precept, the dead can't help living again eventually. It occurs to him that he spends all his time waiting, and that this waiting is his way of being truly constant.

As this idea takes hold, he lurches out of the car, slams the door and hurries down the sloping path that cuts across the forest. He slips through the darkness, trips on roots, flattens himself on the ground and creeps forward on his belly. He slides his hands under the carpet of leaves, his chin chafes on protruding pebbles, and his cheek finds solace in a pillow of moss. Succumbing to the slope, he rolls over and over, full length, then curled into a ball, sometimes folding his limbs in, sometimes stretching them out, flung away from his body; he bounces along, loses his bearings, forgets who he is, his nostrils delighting in the smell of rotting leaves, eyes closed, heart closed too, oddly, because – although he remembers nothing – he does recall learning to get from one place to another between mounds of rock and earth, along dried-up river beds, over bramble bushes. His body harbours memories that his mind has lost.

When he tumbles like this, he becomes ageless. No arthritis restricts his joints, no breathlessness limits his running, his thin torso wraps itself in a soft covering, re-found baby skin, elastic, supple and impervious. In town, he is back to being the fifty-six-year-old man who balks at climbing the stairs; his back creaks and aches if he bends over without thinking first, his hands go red in the cold, his limbs grow stiff if he sits for more than five minutes.

The moon is resting at the top of a chestnut tree, as if on the lip of a chalice. Jerome comes to a stop, slowly inhaling the cool of the night. The air with its rarefied oxygen intoxicates him. He listens to the petals curled up in vegetal sleep and those that, conversely, unfurl to greet nocturnal pollen-gatherers. He feels sheltered; at the mercy of the cold, the rain and insect bites, but sheltered from a more serious threat that he struggles to identify. It is a long-standing threat and he can detect its presence the way animals recognise their predators, without having a name or face to put to them. A threat from before, he thinks, from before the parents, but their coming didn't succeed in thwarting it.

Resting his head on a hollow flint whose smooth concave heart reminds him of a hip joint, he thinks about the time he spent in the forest. It is not unlike the revelation that strikes children, between the ages of four and seven, when they become aware that the world existed before them, that they were nothingness in the universe before they were born. But Jerome doesn't feel the usual terror as he confronts the idea. Unlike children, who refute it as energetically as they explore it, he catches himself toying with it.

I lived alone in a wood, he tells himself, and for the first time he lets his thoughts develop from this starting point. He tries to visualise himself, with the help of photos taken by Annette and Gabriel, to picture what he looked like at three. Green eyes set obliquely in a flat face, blond hair that was already thick, a slightly protruding chin, a mouth ready to bite, a solid wiry body, with no babyish chubbiness. Down on all fours, he prowls between huge tree trunks, sneaks from one bush to another, digs holes to sleep in, to warm himself. He growls, plays with his fingers and toes, watches the birds, crunches on beetles and sucks berries. Jerome knows nothing about this time. He doesn't know how long it lasted or what dangers it posed, but – and this fills him with vertiginous fear – with each new intuition, each image put forward by his mind, he can feel his body, which has forgotten nothing, responding. He is not yet called Jerome, he is sitting in the middle of a clump of bracken, wrapped up warm, solemn, straight-backed, alert to every rustling leaf, every creaking branch. He is waiting. Patches of sunlight shift over the ground. He watches them and smiles.

Jerome stifles a sob. He is crying for the lonely little boy, the lost child, the woodland child. His whole being tenses around this memory which is not truly a memory. He would like to hold the little boy's confident, vigorous body in his arms. All at once sorrow washes over him, as if after an interminable chase. 'I've found you,' the sorrow wails triumphantly. 'You've come back to the woods and you're at my mercy.' But almost immediately, like a wave breaking and then ebbing from the shore, the sorrow draws back, moves away, softens, leaving Jerome more alone than ever.

The moon rises and Jerome recognises the friendly face pitted with craters that used to watch him fall asleep in his shelters made of leaves. The same moon, he thinks. Another terrain, different soil, other trees, but the same moon, my only witness. Slowly, with some difficulty, he gets back to his feet, dusts down his clothes and struggles up the slope towards his car. He is short of breath, his breathing creating spheres of condensation in the dark. He twists an ankle and the pain makes him wince. His hands, scratched by pine needles, are bleeding in places. The cold is eating at his nose, his ears, the tips of his fingers.

Back in his car, he switches on the radio. A woman's voice fills the vehicle. She is describing a total eclipse of the sun, evoking the bluish light cast over upturned faces. It is a childhood memory; she says a few sentences in a foreign language, a Slavic language, and Jerome identifies the word 'kakda'. He doesn't know what it means, but appreciates the sound of it. He writes it down in his notebook and promises himself he will look for a translation in a dictionary.

When he is back home, he turns on all the lights, lights candles, switches on the oven. Anything to get warm. He is frozen to the marrow. His teeth chatter, he feels frightened, powerless. The three-year-old child, the woodland child, has taken hold of him and is asking for explanations. How am I going to eat? he asks Jerome. And what about sleeping, without blankets or a bed? How am I going to pee? There are no toilets, no potty, nothing. How do I wash? How do I get warm? How do I stop crying when I've got no one to cuddle me?

Jerome shakes his head, as if to dispel a nightmare. He is ashamed of his self-pity. He feels mawkish, and is not best pleased with this invasion from such an easily identified ghost of the past. A fortnight ago he heard radio listeners talking about rediscovering themselves, the salutary effects of delving into the past, the tenderness they had learnt to feel for the child within them. A velvet-voiced man with a smooth lisp made comments, quoting Freud and telling the story of the Wolf Man, mentioning *Gradiva*. Jerome found it painful, couldn't make any notes on the page he had pulled out, wounded by so much sincerity, by this tide of outpourings and the atmosphere of general compassion. Bunch of wimps, he thought, not expanding on this. Nothing but wimps. And he threw the piece of paper in the bin. At the time, Armand was still alive.

He hears the bedroom door open and rushes out into the corridor.

'Marina!' he calls.

It feels an age since he said her name.

His daughter looks at him amazed, graceful as a fennec fox.

'Marina, look at this!'

She stays there in the corridor, motionless. Frowns. Jerome remembers using this tactic to deflect her moods when she was little. 'Marina, look at this,' he would say, knowing that the child's curiosity was stronger than anything else. 'Look at this, I've found a snail! Look at this, the moon's all orange! Look at this, there's a programme about orang-utans on TV!' The enthusiasm he injected into it persuaded her to put her tantrum off till later, to make the most of the current magic, the surprise, the find.

'Come here, my darling,' he adds more steadily, reaching a hand out to her.

Marina takes a step back, tilts her head to the ceiling to drive back her tears and walks slowly towards her father.

They hug, and a few seconds later, they cry.

'My love, my little love,' he murmurs, stroking her head.

He sits on the sofa and takes her on his knee.

'It's awful,' he says. 'It's not fair.'

Jerome feels Marina's tears trickling down his neck. He pats her back, hugs her to him. He would like to tell her a story, like when she was little. Once upon a time there was a boy who lived in the woods. But he can't say a thing. His jaws are welded together. They stay like this a long time, buffeted by the waves, forsaken, like a raft lost in the middle of a demented ocean.

I wish I understood too, he says inside his head, finding it impossible to talk. I'd like to find some meaning and be able to explain it to you, the way parents are supposed to for their children. I'd like to give you a bit of hope, tell you you're young and beautiful and the most wonderful girl, and that there's a long, exciting life in store for you. You'll have to believe me when I tell you that one day you'll hold your child in your arms and nothing else will matter any more, that the two of you will be the whole world, the universe. Trust me. This tragedy won't swallow you up. You'll get back on your feet, you'll live again.

Something in Marina's body relaxes, gives in. Jerome daren't move. She has gone to sleep. He listens to her breathing, spiked with sobs. He strokes her back, smoothes out the tattered edges of her pain, quietly sings an old rhyme that he used to lull her with when she woke in the night, terrified by a nightmare. A candle on the coffee table sputters. Jerome smiles. Everything's alive, he thinks, dazed.

'Shush, she's sleeping,' he tells Rosy, opening the front door to her.

He didn't let her ring the bell. As soon as he heard her moped on the gravel he lay his daughter's head on a cushion and got up to stop the noise waking her.

'That's good,' Rosy nods. 'She needs to rest.'

She offers Jerome her wide Manchurian smile.

'You can still stay, if you'd like,' he suggests.

'Okay.'

She hangs her helmet and coat on a peg in the hallway and walks ahead of Jerome down the corridor to the kitchen. He admires her heft, her solid grip on things, the touching swing of her obese form.

'Shall we have a little coffee, then?' she says conspiratorially, stationing herself beside the hob.

'No, it's too late.'

'What have you done to your hands?' she blurts, staring at his scratches.

'Nothing. Nothing at all. I did some gardening.'

'Have you disinfected them?'

Jerome wants to ask Rosy if she has a boyfriend, but is worried she'll take it the wrong way, will think he's coming on to her. So he asks her what she is planning to do in life.

Rosy takes a pouch from her bag and lays out its contents on the table.

'Mountain climber,' she whispers.

Jerome is not sure whether this is a joke. He waits to hear more.

'Or a prima ballerina. I can't make up my mind,' she adds, putting a cigarette paper into a rolling machine. 'Do you mind?' she asks Jerome, gesturing at him with the little brown ball that she starts crumbling without waiting for his go-ahead.

Drugs, he thinks. It's drugs. He doesn't dare admit that he's never smoked. He hopes it's not dangerous. He steadies himself with the thought that it's probably not heroine. He wonders briefly what he did with his youth. Exactly which monastery did he hide away in all through the seventies?

'Aren't you a bit young for that?' he ventures.

'Young? Shit *is* pretty much a young thing,' she says in a teacherly voice.

'And do your parents know?'

'My parents?' Rosy replies, her face suddenly closed. 'I'll ask their opinion when they've got one. It'll do you good,' she insists. 'You'll see.'

'What about Marina? Will you give her some?'

'No. No way. With grief you have to live the whole thing properly. No drink, no weed. Nothing. You have to take it full in the face, suffer all the way.'

How's this girl found time to become an expert on the subject? Jerome admires her self-assurance, her determination.

84

He wants to know if she has already been through a similar tragedy, but instead he asks:

'Wouldn't you like to be a doctor? Rather than a mountain climber or a dancer. I think you'd make a very good doctor.'

'Me?' Rosy exclaims, stifling a laugh. 'Me?' she says again, eyes wide.

'Why not?'

'I'm doing the L baccalaureate, in case you'd forgotten. L for Loser-at-maths.'

'So is Marina doing the L baccalaureate too?'

Rosy stops laughing.

'Which planet are you on? You don't even know which group your daughter's in? You must have signed the papers, the forms with her request and the decision from the staff, didn't you?'

Jerome doesn't remember. He shrugs.

'I think her mother took care of all that,' he says eventually, instantly ashamed of how feeble it sounds.

'What the hell's going on with parents these days?' Rosy flares up. 'Have you all lost the plot or something? I thought mine were serious cases, but—'

'Okay, listen,' Jerome interrupts her tartly. 'If you came here to tell me how to behave, you can leave.'

Rosy doesn't budge. Still staring at Jerome insolently, affectionately, she carefully rolls her spliff and lights it.

'Maybe I *will* become a doctor,' she says, handing him the joint. 'If it would make you happy.'

Jerome takes it, inhales awkwardly, coughs, then inhales again.

'Sometimes,' Rosy goes on, 'we can't cope with what we're meant to be coping with. Do you know what I mean? Like now, being with Marina. No one can actually do it, we don't know how to do it. It's at times like that that I smoke. I'm sure there are some things in life that don't do any good at all. For Marina it's really important that we're with her, but for us it's crap, it just shouldn't be there on the register.'

'The register?' asks Jerome, feeling his cheeks relaxing, melting, dribbling over his shoulders. 'What's this register, then?'

Rosy taps her temple with the tip of her index finger and repeats the word: 'The register.'

She takes the joint back and smokes again, rolling her slanting eyes and fluttering her eyelashes.

The register, thinks Jerome, where everything is registered, the memory cave.

'Do you know what *I* do when things are too difficult?' Rosy asks. 'When I can't cope and even weed doesn't help?'

Jerome shakes his head and takes the joint she is offering again.

'I head off into the future.'

'How do you mean?'

'With a time machine. We've all got one inside us. You just have to use it. All you do is think: in a week, it'll be over. Or: in a year, I'll be over it. Or, if it's more serious: when I'm old, it won't matter at all.'

'But sometimes we go the wrong way, don't we? We go to the past instead of the future. Do you think we use the same machine to go to the past?'

Rosy considers this, takes the joint, inhales slowly, tilting her big round head to one side like a sunflower.

'No, there isn't a machine for the past. That's where I don't agree with Jules Verne and the other guys like him. You don't need a gadget to go to the past, we do it the whole time, quite naturally. It's like time's on a hill: for the past it's downhill, so you don't need to pedal. But the future's uphill, so you need an engine.'

'Vroom, vroom!' exclaims Jerome.

Rosy bursts out laughing.

'Vroom, vroom!' she says too. 'By car. Destination: next year. Right, let's have a look, what's going on next year?'

She closes her eyes, holding her hands out across the table.

'Ignition!' she murmurs.

'Ignition!' replies Jerome, reaching his battered hands to touch the tips of Rosy's fingers.

'I can see swirling leaves,' she announces in what she imagines a medium's voice would be like. 'I can see a chubby

87

girl re-taking the last year of school, doing an S baccalaureate so she can become a doctor. I can see an estate agent smiling in the doorway of his office. There's a woman beside him, a very pretty woman with a basket over her arm. I can see Marina smiling at the gate to the cemetery. There's a boy carrying her bag.'

'Why isn't she carrying it herself? Is she ill?'

'No!' Rosy exclaims, suddenly opening her eyes. 'She's pregnant!'

'Already?'

'Already,' Rosy confirms, stubbing out her spliff in astonishment. 'Weird, isn't it? Did you like it?'

'I don't feel very good,' says Jerome. 'I want to be sick.'

'That's normal, visions make you feel giddy. You need to lie down. You go to bed, I'll take care of Marina.'

Jerome stands up, reeling slightly. He leans on the door frame. Everything is spinning round him.

'Hey, Rosy,' he says, pasty-mouthed. 'Is it actually possible to switch from a literary baccalaureate to a scientific one?'

'No,' she replies, 'I don't think so.'

Rosy's voice is a bit shaky as she says this. Jerome should be consoling her, should find an instant solution, buttonhole the local authorities, lay siege to the Ministry of Education. But instead of this, he goes off to his room without a word and collapses onto his bed.

*

During the night, Jerome hears noises: a clapper knocking on a cracked bell, a snail easing in and out of its shell, logs falling on sand, all amplified and molten. Every time he tries to lift his head to work out where the sound is coming from and what is making it, a cone of felt flattens itself over his forehead, pinning him to the pillow. Through his eyelids he can make out glowing lights, shadows, hectic mayflies around a light bulb. He wants to open his eyes, but his lashes are stuck together. 'With honey,' a dream voice whispers. With honey? he asks, half-conscious. Honey on his eyelashes. The explanation seems startlingly logical to him; he accepts it and goes back to sleep.

The young, like sprites ten times more mischievous in the silence after dark, are busying themselves around the house. Rosy is talking about Clementine. Zoe and Mathias have come to do a shift and she is telling them Jerome asked her some questions.

'What did he want to know?' asks Zoe.

'He was off his head,' says Rosy. 'So sweet. He told me I'm like a pony. I kind of like it. He wants me to be a doctor. He said he wanted to pay for me to do my studies.'

She is crying with laughter.

'He's in love with you,' Zoe announces.

'No he isn't. He was just off his head and being kind. And afterwards he asked if I knew Clementine.'

'So?'

'Well, I had to explain what Goth meant because he'd never heard of one. I told him about the ring with the skull, the scarring, all that stuff. And anyway, it was über-weird because his hands were all scratched, like he'd had a go at them with a razor blade.'

'Why does he want to know about Clementine?' Mathias intervenes.

'I dunno. Because she's gone. Because of Armand.'

'She's not gone because of Armand,' Zoe corrects her.

'No, that's not what I'm saying. I'm saying he's interested in her firstly because she's gone and secondly because of Armand, seeing as he is too – well, you get the picture.'

'But what's the connection?' asks Mathias.

'Isn't one. But, like I said, he was off his head. He went to sleep at half past six in the evening, like a baby.'

'What about Marina?' asks Zoe.

'Marina's sleeping too.'

'Shall we have ourselves a beer and get out of here?' Mathias suggests.

'And dance for five minutes,' adds Zoe.

They execute the programme with great precision. Bottle tops off, bottles clinked together, drinking straight from the neck, tramp of heavy-soled shoes on the tiles to a rhythm emitted by headphones clamped to their ears.

*

Jerome wakes with a start at three o'clock in the morning. He went to sleep on top of his covers, with the window open; his teeth are chattering. As he tries to get to the door, he bangs into a table. He inspects the house, tries to remember the evening. Marina is no longer on the sofa. The candle wax has trickled over the furniture, the wicks are drowning in paraffin. There's a smell of cold, cardboard and yeast. The kitchen has changed. It's not untidy, it's not dirty, it's different, as if a large family appropriated it for the space of an evening.

Jerome nudges the door to Marina's bedroom. She is asleep in her bed, a flowery shawl laid over her duvet. Someone's taken care of her, he thinks, comforted. He remembers Cousinet's advice: we have to look after teenagers, they're fragile; like bonsais, they need constant attention.

Marina has grown up without his noticing. She has never caused him the least headache. He remembers every time his own mother, Annette, wanted to buy a plant from a garden centre she would ask whether it was hardy. She had a peculiarly suspicious way of asking the question, staring at the salesman or woman through lowered eyes, as if to say: don't you go giving me the sales patter on this. Jerome wasn't sure what she meant by hardy. Wasn't there someone called Hardy who got kissed? But he couldn't remember ever seeing her kiss her plants. Then, one day, most likely because he looked particularly perplexed when Annette asked this favourite question, she leant towards him and explained:

'Hardy, my darling, means they can cope with all conditions. With a hardy plant, even if you don't water it, it manages to capture water with its leaves, and if it burns in the sun, it recovers overnight. Hardy means something that doesn't die. That means a lot to me, my little man, do you see? I don't want them to die.'

Perhaps, unlike friends her own age, and thanks to her grandmother's unspoken blessings from beyond the grave, Marina has avoided the common lot. She is the exception: a hardy plant among bonsais.

6

Little dog
Little cat
And a bim and a bam and a rata-tat-tat
The dog says bow-ow
The cat says miaow!

Jerome is singing quietly to himself as he waits outside his office. He hops from one foot to the other to stop the cold seeping into him. After a few minutes he realises how stupid his ditty is. He doesn't know where it's from. It's the sort of thing Annette used to invent when he was little. Sometimes he would ask her for a real song, 'Frère Jacques' or 'Hey Diddle Diddle', but she didn't know any.

'Everyone knows "Frère Jacques",' he grumbled, thinking his mother odd, not liking the aura of mystery around her.

He envied his school friends whose mothers were young,

lipsticked, chic, normal, the ones who did sing 'Frère Jacques' and 'Hey Diddle Diddle'.

When he was eight years old, he asked for a big compendium of nursery rhymes for Christmas. Annette complied with this whim and, with the help of the LP slotted into the cover, she tried to learn the classics her son insisted on. But it was no good, they wouldn't go in. 'Jack and Jill went over the hill, to sketch the farmer's daughter.' She more or less respected the tunes, but seemed to find it impossible not to distort the words. 'Row, row, row your boat gently down the stream. Tippety, toppety, slippety, sloppety, you fall in then you scream,' she would sing in a nasal, high-pitched and very distinct voice. It sounded nice, but it wasn't right.

'He loves the most banal things!' Annette used to say with a laugh if asked to describe Jerome's character. 'Bangers and mash, bouquets of roses, milk chocolate, piano music, the colour red, detective books.'

She was proud of this list, which she recited like an artist unveiling his latest work, full of courage and apprehension.

As soon as he was old enough to understand that 'banal' was hardly a flattering term, Jerome made a point of modifying his inclinations. He forced himself to like calves' liver, buttercups, dark chocolate, oboe music, pistachio green and symbolist poetry. This meant that, by the age of thirteen, he had unwittingly cut himself off from a whole generation of teenagers who viewed him as peculiar. They called him the intellectual, the snob and the old man. It didn't matter, though – it suited him better being unconventional. The solitude he needed to live his other life as a wild child was the most important thing. It wasn't a good idea having too many friends if, like him, you spent whole days scratching at the earth in the undergrowth, listening to tree trunks creaking, studying stripes of sunlight on tree roots, and gathering the dew collected in the crook of a leaf to drink it drop by drop.

'I'm late, like the White Rabbit!' exclaims Vilno Smith, standing squarely in front of him, her lumberjacket open to show a shapeless pullover with an incredible plunging neckline.

What's this business about a rabbit? Jerome wonders as he puts his hand out to shake hers.

'I don't mind waiting,' he says.

There is so much truth in this statement that he is briefly stunned, his gaze captivated by his client's sturdy collar bones, her warrior-like chest with visible ribs and her small, cheeky breasts.

'That's pretty rare,' she says. 'Very rare, these days, someone who's not in a hurry.'

She nods admiringly.

'You're quite a phenomenon!' she adds, amused, her great animal head breaking into a sunny smile.

Jerome isn't listening to what she's saying. He is looking at her as if he has to decide what species this tall, vigorous woman belongs to. I've never met anyone like her, he thinks, trying to pinpoint what it is that distinguishes her so radically from other specimens. Her height, the lack of make-up, the way she dresses, that air of independence, of autonomy, as if she belongs to no one and is responsible for nothing. He is not sure he likes it. Facing her requires a degree of effort. But what sort of effort? An effort of imagination, because he gets the feeling that usual codes of conversation will be no help at all with this foreigner.

There was a time, not that long ago, when country cottages were selling like hot cakes as holiday homes for people from neighbouring countries, and he had dealings with German, Dutch, Belgian and English people, but that was different. Wealthy buyers saw him as merely an intermediary, a devoted flunky to be treated considerately thanks to an aristocratic aesthetic, but they never went so far as to think he harboured a human heart or mind.

Jerome feels that something about Vilno Smith communicates directly with him, as if she is as interested in who he is as she is in the properties he plans to show her.

'Are we going to see the pig house?' she asks.

'That's right. The piggery. Would you like to follow me by car?'

'I'd very much like to follow you by car, my dear man, but the drawback is I don't possess such a vehicle.'

Where did you learn to speak? he wants to ask her.

'Well, I'll drive you, then. We could go on foot, but it would take half a day.'

He has often walked the route. He wouldn't be loath to do it with her. Thanks to her giant strides, they would carve a nice straight wake into the easterly light, with her at the prow and him at the stern, protected from gusts of morning wind by the wings of her open jacket.

She insists on sitting in the back of the car. She has always dreamt of having a chauffeur.

'If it makes you happy,' he says, immediately regretting this sarcastic comment.

But she takes it well.

'Yes it makes me very happy, Monsieur Dampierre. Dampierre, surely that sounds like 'dans pierre' – in stone? You must have an ancestor who was walled up alive, or perhaps he was a colossus, a man with incredible strength, so people said he was made of stone—'

'I'm a foundling,' he interrupts.

She doesn't react. He looks in the rear-view mirror and sees his passenger's golden irises focused on his own. She is studying him, without a word.

That shut her up, he thinks triumphantly. But it is a short-lived victory. He would like her to give some sort of response. He realises, although he doesn't know why, that he really needs her to react to this revelation. Maybe she didn't hear properly, he thinks. Or she doesn't know the expression. Maybe it doesn't mean anything in her language. He decides to carry on.

'My parents aren't my real parents, or rather they *weren't* my real parents. They died more than thirty years ago. They adopted me. The name they gave me isn't *my* ancestors' name, but theirs…'

He breaks off abruptly, paralysed by the whole question of ancestors. It suddenly seems absurd to him that his father could have inherited the name from anyone at all. Annette and Gabriel Dampierre – something about the way it's assembled just doesn't ring true. He looks in the rear-view mirror again. Vilno Smith's eyes are turned towards the window at the moment. She is looking at the succession of rusty brown, black and khaki fields. Jerome stays silent.

'Is it much further?' she asks eventually.

'Yes, no. Actually, I took a wrong turning.'

'Did you take a long-cut?'

'Pardon?'

'A long-cut, it's the opposite of a short-cut. I'm not in a hurry either, you know. Before, I never had any time and I did stacks of things. Now, I've got lots of time and do hardly anything.'

'And what do you prefer?'

'I prefer now. I always prefer now. We're better off now, aren't we?'

'How do you mean, better off?'

'Better off than when we were young, when we wore jeans that were too tight, better off than when we got married. I used to have a timber company. I oversaw fifty-seven woodcutters. I made quite a lot of money. My husband made even more, but he sold buttons.'

'Buttons?' Jerome asks, afraid he misheard.

'Yes, buttons. Unbelievable, isn't it? Mother of pearl shirt buttons. Very pretty little things, but slightly ridiculous too. We didn't really see eye to eye.'

'Because of the buttons?'

'No. Perhaps a bit, but not only that. One time when I went to London on business, I took the Tube. At the time I had enough money to afford a chauffeur, a real one, but I preferred taking the Tube, to see people's faces. Old men's eyebrows, as long as head hair; women's hairstyles, like meringues; and the shoes, the shoes... So there I was on the Tube and it was pretty full. I was standing, and at Green Park a whole group of tourists got into the carriage. I took a step back and felt a clenched fist in the back of my knee; it was the man sitting just behind me. I didn't move, neither did he. All the way to Victoria I cupped his hand there. It was the most sensuous experience I'd had in fifteen years. When I went home to Norfolk, I left my husband.'

'What about the man on the Tube?'

'What man on the Tube?'

'The one… with the fist.'

'I don't even know what he looked like. I stepped off the train without looking. No, who gives a damn about the man on the Tube! It's not him that's important. It's my husband that matters, my husband whose hands were never in the right place.'

What about you? Do you always know where to put your hands? he would like to ask, in defence of the inept husband, of all husbands and all inept people. Basically, he's had enough of these women who know more about everything than anyone else, who criticise and always find fault with everything. What advantage have they got? Who taught them to live any better than us, who told them the secrets that make them full of themselves from morning till night?

'So you were abandoned, then?' Vilno Smith enquires, just as Jerome is parking on the dirt track that leads to the piggery.

'Pardon?' he says, still irritated by the anecdote about the Tube.

'You say your parents adopted you. So I deduced that, before that, someone must have abandoned you. Your real mother – what's the word they use? Genetic? Biological? She got rid of you.'

'That doesn't matter,' says Jerome, getting out of the car.

'Why not?'

'It's like the man on the Tube. I don't know what my mother looked like.'

'Almost certainly quite a lot like you,' she says, pleased with this find.

Not realising he is doing it, Jerome puts his hand to his face, his cheeks, his chin, mouth, nostrils, under his eyes. He fingers his mother's face through his own. No wrinkles, high cheekbones, almond eyes, slightly yellow skin in the middle of the forehead.

'I've had seven abortions,' Vilno tells him. 'Not a day goes by that I don't think of the children I could have had. What they would have looked like. There would be eight of them in all now, if I'd been a fervent Catholic. And, in a sense, I am a fervent Catholic, given that I think about them all the time. But, in another sense, I'm the opposite of a fervent Catholic because I'm in favour, massively in favour, of abortion. I'm in favour of every kind of contraceptive, but, at the same time, I think about the dead babies. We're not supposed to say that, to call them babies, it's politically incorrect. I'd never say it to another woman. I say it to myself. And I said it to you because you're a man. Because I'm sure you've never had an abortion. I'm sure it won't hurt you.'

My wife had an abortion, thinks Jerome. Paula didn't want another child when she was pregnant the second time. She said Marina was all she needed, that she wouldn't know how to share herself. She asked what I thought. As if I had to be the baby's lawyer. I didn't know what to say. When she came home after the procedure, I realised I did think something, but it was too late.

'We chat well together, the two of us, don't you think?' Vilno says as she walks along the path, the sides of her jacket spread like ray's wings.

Jerome doesn't answer. He feels embarrassed, unworthy. He watches her stepping swiftly over the barbed-wire fence, wonders why she didn't go through the wooden gate covered in lichen. He copies her. A metal spike sinks into his trouser leg and tears the fabric, making a delicious noise that he hopes his client missed. The morning sidles its icy hand along his thigh.

'Wait for me!' he cries, worried she might break a window pane to get in.

Vilno Smith barges through the door, not listening to him; the padlock releases, he has no idea why.

'It's not locked,' she calls from inside the cob-walled cottage.

When he goes in to join her, he is surprised by the sudden total darkness. His eyes struggle to make out the walls, floor and ceiling. He can hear wisps of straw rustling overhead.

'I'm upstairs,' calls a voice.

He looks, fumbles. His hands find the rungs of a ladder. He climbs up and a trapdoor opens above his head. The morning sun is streaming through a skylight in the east-facing gable.

Feathers and wheat dust dance in the oblique ray of light. The floor is strewn with droppings from birds, mice and flies. Can it be, thinks Jerome, can it be that time has gone into reverse? We're children and we're playing in an abandoned house. We keep no secrets from each other. We go off together to hay lofts and pretend to smoke by slipping the tiny golden shafts between our lips. We breathe in deeply. So little air reaches us that our heads spin. We play injured soldiers, then mummies and daddies, lost adventurers, doctors and nurses. We glory in the world before the Fall, we don't know we're naked.

'Welcome to the master bedroom!' cries Vilno Smith. 'This is my bedroom. I've got feathers to make an eiderdown, animal droppings to improve the insulation. No refurbishment required, as the agencies say. That is what they say, isn't it? Mr Dampierre?'

She has a particular way of pronouncing his name, the name that has never felt as if it belonged to him. She breaks it down: 'dans' and then 'pierre', giving it a meaning it has never had for him. That's a foreigner's gift, hearing sounds where, since their early childhood, native speakers hear only words.

He smiles and is amazed by the sensations it produces. As if his face has lost this precious form of expression and he is finally finding it once more after a very long time. He remembers laughing with Paula and Rosy, but this is different. Laughter is convulsive, sharp, nervy. A smile soothes.

'My, what pretty teeth you have!' says Vilno Smith. 'Isn't that what Little Red Riding Hood says to the wolf?'

'I don't know. I don't know *Little Red Riding Hood.*'

Vilno Smith bursts out laughing.

'You don't know *Little Red Riding Hood*? But everyone knows it, it's part of western childhood, universal upbringing, the trio that sums everything up better than Oedipus. Little girl, wolf, grandmother.'

Jerome doesn't understand a word she's saying. The woman's exhausting. She's too tall, too lively, too earnest. She never stops talking, has no sense of propriety. She is sitting cross-legged on the filthy floor, playfully wafting tiny feathers in the air.

'I know the story,' he says eventually. 'But I don't remember the exact words.'

He's lying. He knows that Little Red Riding Hood says: 'What big teeth you have', and that the wolf replies: 'All the better to eat you with'. He refuses to fall into such a naively set trap. He doesn't want to play or pretend. He knows where that ends up. No way he'll let himself get drawn into that. Poppycock and fiddlesticks, his mind sings. He's not ready to have fun, he's supposed to be stricken. Yes, that's the exact feeling. He feels respect for his own stricken state. His pain constitutes a sort of sacred field. It expects cult status from which nothing can distract him.

He climbs back down, dusts himself off and walks out of the piggery.

In the garden – where summer grass has grown up, then yellowed and wilted – palm-sized horizontal spiders' webs map out a circuit of fatal trampolines for midges. Jerome walks away, trying not to crush any of them. He admires the early-morning work of these weavers who hunt only while dew is on the ground. There, he thinks to himself. That's what I like. Observing nature, knowing the habits of insects and birds, catching heifers spontaneously mounting each other, seeing a hare daydreaming halfway across a path. We'd have got on so well together, Armand and me. We'd have planted and dug up, pricked out and taken cuttings, without a word.

He misses the boy's silence, his gentleness and steadfastness. He catches himself making an impossible calculation. Let's say Marina loved Armand a hundred times more than I did. Then her grief must be a hundred times worse than mine. He is completely floored by the enormity of this pain. He can't see how a body, his daughter's body, can hold so much. He's overwhelmed by the absurdity of his own thought processes.

His shoes are soaked, his trousers too. He feels powerless and completely disorientated. Sentences come to him about how difficult it is living with women, the fight it entails, the feelings you have to keep showing, the pathetic little games of seduction, and then afterwards: the dolls' house, making babies.

Making them, yes, fine, it's all fireworks, pride and superpowers, but after that you feel knocked back, slowed down by all those endless, boring, repetitive tasks. The way you talk to each other, as if to a colleague, to a nurse, to a dog. And yet, four years after Marina was born, he longed for a little boy, another baby, with a fat tummy, chubby cheeks and a ready laugh. Paula left the choice to him. She didn't particularly want one, she said, as if she were talking about chocolate mousse on a menu, but she'd let herself be tempted if he wanted it badly enough. Wanting a child, what could that possibly mean? Children happen and there it is, you shouldn't even ask the question. He was quite happy for Paula's breasts to swell again, quite happy to have the sour smell of milk on the sheets, the snuggly tunnel you make at night to lull a body not much longer than your forearm. But another child? Why? Why just one? Why not twelve? He was too slow. It was only afterwards that nostalgia gripped him. A little boy, all sweet and cuddly. Or even a girl. Too late. They never talked about it again. They had so little time, and as soon as they had any, they succumbed to exhaustion. The exhaustion of being together, of looking at each other and constructing something.

One afternoon, on the way back from a house visit, he stopped his car outside a rural bar to have a beer out on the terrace. The sun was shining and spring madness was infecting budding blossom. A woman arrived in a Citroën with 75 at the end of its number plate. A Parisian. She was exactly as you would imagine one, faithful to the caricature: unpleasant, in a hurry, elegant, sure of herself. There was only one table outside. She eyed Jerome furiously: he'd nicked her place.

'We can share, if you'd like,' he suggested.

She ordered a beer and sat opposite him, a small smile on her lips. He felt handsome, strong, absolutely irresistible.

He had no idea what he could say to her, what sort of conversation a Parisian would like. He was more frightened of demeaning himself than anything else. So he said nothing. They raised their glasses and clinked them together in silence and mentally made love a dozen times.

When he arrived home, Paula greeted him with: '*I* had to empty the bins yet again.'

Jerome thought they needed to change something, that life could in all probability be nicer. But he couldn't work out how to go about it.

'Look, a stork!' cries Vilno Smith behind him.

Jerome looks up and sees the white bird with its anthracite-edged wings cleaving the blue sky.

'What are you up to, sitting on the ground like that?' she asks.

'Nothing, waiting for you. Would you like to see the other building?'

'No, it suits me perfectly. It's exactly what I was looking for.'

'Impossible.'

'No it's not. Why do you say that?'

'Because it never happens. Not on a first visit. And even then, when people eventually find what they're looking for, there's always some snag, some drawback, some regret. There isn't a well here, for example.'

'But there's something better than a well – there's a marsh.'

'Where's that, then?'

'Over there.' She waves towards the east. 'I can smell marshland. I saw some gorse from the skylight.'

'There isn't a marsh. I live here, you know, I do a lot of walking. There isn't a marsh.'

'Yes there is. Or there *was* one, but it comes down to the same thing.'

'Why do you like marshes so much?'

'I'm not revealing everything. I need to take things gently with you. You're a little country bumpkin, narrow-minded.'

She says this with no malice, like an ethnologist establishing the facts.

She's right, Jerome thinks, although he doesn't see how he could be seen to agree. He would like to be aggressive in return, to tell her that the stork she thought she saw was actually a grey heron, and what she thinks is a marsh is merely an artificial pond dug between three quarries.

'It's not just because we're out in the country,' he says. 'You get a bit of everything in the country like anywhere else. There are idiots, clever people and eccentrics, exactly like anywhere else.'

'Then why is it?'

Jerome doesn't answer this question.

'It needs at least 30,000 euros spending on it,' he estimates. 'There's no water or electricity. This piggery's a bottomless pit financially.'

'Is that your sales strategy?'

'What?'

'What you did then, running it down, is that a strategy?'

'No, it's the truth. It's what it says on my file. Sale price: 40,000 euros. Minimum building costs: 25,000 euros.'

'And how did they cope before?'

'What do you mean before?'

'In the days when there was never any water or electricity in houses. In the eighteenth century, and even the nineteenth.'

She won't let up on me, thinks Jerome. She wants to have me surrounded. First with her confidences, and now with her history lessons. I've got to get away, I need to make some notes in my notebook. I want to be alone. A tree, the woods, running. Alone.

'We're heading back,' he says, standing up and going towards the car. 'I've got other meetings.'

Jerome pats his pockets, looking for his key. It isn't there.

Not in his jacket, nor his coat, nor his trousers. It's slipped out, disappeared.

'What's going on?' Vilno Smith asks.

He swears. Kicks the car tyres, crawls along the barbed-wire fence on all fours, searches through the dead, flattened yellow grass. He sinks his fingers into clumps of moss and mud, underground dormitories where larvae wait, huddled together, for fine weather.

'Can't you find your keys?'

Without answering, he stands up and sets off down the path, walking away from the piggery and his car, crossing the road and cutting across the fields. He doesn't look back, doesn't want to know whether she is following him, convinced that she is on his heels, and resigned to enduring her assault. Sometimes he runs, then slows down before he is out of breath, taking the time to savour the light. A bright yellow paintbrush daubs the late apples with an almost fluorescent tint against a threatening sky loaded with steel. The first fat, sporadic raindrops heavy as cherries start to fall while the sun still lights up the fields, honouring every pebble with a gleaming pointed hat. It feels like a summer storm, windless. The rain falls straight down, hard. No thunder, though, no lightning.

Jerome is walking very slowly now. He knows he can't fight. That he will be soaked whatever he does. Vilno Smith was wise enough not to follow him. She must have taken refuge in the house while she waits for him to get back or for a breakdown man to arrive. She has the practical sense Jerome so lacks. She looked at the sky and read the meteorological future inscribed in the grey of the clouds.

But maybe she got lost. At the point where the path forks, where an old milestone stands with a great fat snail sliding over its foot, even in hot weather. The snail follows an orbital track, its presence inexplicable, its constancy an unexpected gift. Jerome took the time to check the gastropod was there, on duty, as he veered off to the right.

She must have gone left. It's the more obvious path, wide and carving prettily through the hedges, except it doesn't actually lead anywhere. It used to serve the back entrance to a chateau, but the owner set light to the place fifteen years ago to get his hands on the insurance. Jerome was lucky to have visited the chateau before the blaze. Painted beams: dragons' tongues; ribbons weaving between pieces of fruit pitted by woodworm; pillars framing idylls featuring shepherds and chambermaids, stags and does, and even, over a smaller doorway which he had identified as the entrance to Bluebeard's grim chamber, a satyr and nymph with long rabbit's ears. Most likely a fake, a pastiche, a joke created by a mildly pornographic amateur painter. The fire broke out, as these things do, in the middle of the night. The following evening there was nothing left. Today, when you reach the end of the path, a sign – complete with a peculiarly menacing exclamation mark – prohibits going any further. Jerome doesn't know who put it there or why. There is no danger of any sort, nothing to steal or even to see, except perhaps for the lie perpetrated by the drunken and solitary heir, who traded centuries of romance for a few years of drink.

Vilno Smith will be sheltering as best she can from the drips, he thinks, sitting between the venerable paws of a vast horse chestnut. She'll be cursing him, weeping with fury, catching her death. And he's responsible.

In his guilty musings, Jerome never imagines Vilno's hand closing round the car key in the pocket of her jacket. He can't picture her snuggled in the warmth accumulated by the hay all through the summer. She let herself into the other building which has a sweet smell of rotten apples. She's laughing at her practical joke, pretending to chastise herself because of the rain knifing the ground and seeping into the poor estate agent's clothes, down his neck and into the small of his back.

'Ha!' she snaps victoriously towards the roof, which is leaking fine streams of water.

Her cry wakens a Tengmalm's owl sleeping in the rafters. The furious bird shakes its wings, loses a few feathers, moves fifty centimetres along the beam and goes back to sleep.

When he arrives home via the small road at the back, Jerome's cheeks are flushed scarlet. He can't tell whether he's hot or cold. His body is weighed down by waterlogged clothes.

He hasn't met a soul. He slips in through the small doorway in the north wall that is never locked, and squelches through the bed of dead flowers. All at once his foot sinks in deep as if drawn down by quicksand. The moist soil swallows his ankle, sucks on his calf. Jerome jerks on it and falls forwards. He decides to get into the house through the basement and to change in the utility room. Marina mustn't hear him or see him in this state. There's something uncomfortable in his shoe, digging into his heel. As soon as he is inside he gets undressed, right next to the boiler, and throws his muddy things into the washing machine. He is surprised to hear a crystalline tinkling sound. Something dropped from his shoe and is lying on the white tiled floor: a shining silver ring with a skull-and-crossbones design.

7

'I've lost you,' says Inspector Cousinet.

These words wake Jerome from his reverie. His mind had drifted off for a moment. He finds it happens more and more often.

It is night time. They are in the Bar des Sports, drinking beer with a golden glow that perfectly mimics the colour of the street lights in the square. Without realising it, Jerome lost himself in this chromatic coincidence. He allowed his eye to be drawn by the large yellow bulb attached to a post above the chemist's, and the lamplight ricocheted all the way to his glass. He takes a sip, trying to win some time to remember the thread of the conversation, struggles, knitting his brows. He instinctively brings his hand to his jacket pocket where he has put his notebook, as if the answer were written in there.

'This isn't a standard enquiry,' Cousinet goes on. 'As I said, I've retired. It's a sort of professional deformity. I've got so used to resolving enigmas that that's how I see life. There's no suspect, not even a crime. Just the mystery of these disappearances. Have you noticed that, in a starry sky, it's very easy to spot the plough, probably because someone once told you the constellation looks like a saucepan with a slightly curved handle? Well, in the same way that you can't help yourself seeing a saucepan in the sky, I can make out a pattern in these cases, and once I've seen it, I can't take my eyes off it. Death isn't always a factor – I mean, it doesn't explain everything. People settle for that far too often, and far too quickly. The young don't die, they run away.'

'You mean to say Armand...' Jerome manages hesitantly.

'No. I'm generalising. I'm explaining my theory. Have I told you about my theory?'

Jerome doesn't remember anything. A theory about death? About the young?

'Well, I didn't go into much detail,' Cousinet acknowledges. 'I'm so worried I'll bore people with it that I don't do much more than mention it. But I get the feeling you'd be interested. Am I wrong?'

Jerome shakes his head, to be polite. What *am* I interested in? he wonders.

'The young in the country!' exclaims Cousinet, beaming. 'It's tough for them. Their world's too limited. They've all known each other since they were children. There's not enough shuffling. And, nowadays, people need shuffling. In the old days, people didn't know there was a world outside their own. What am I saying? *A* world? Masses of worlds, that start where theirs ends. Now they have TV and the Internet. It sounds like a cliché, but it's important. The young think about love; meeting someone is a big preoccupation. The problem is that here, unlike in big cities, the sexual possibilities are very restricted. Do you see what I mean?'

Sexual possibilities... Jerome thinks to himself, fighting to break away from contemplating the luminous gold trapped at the bottom of his glass.

'Think back to your schooldays. Were you a boarder?'

'No.'

'It doesn't make much difference. Whether you were boarding or not, how many pretty girls were there for you to choose from?'

'Secondary schools weren't mixed in those days,' Jerome points out.

'That's true, quite right. But the schools were in adjoining buildings. You knew the entire female population, didn't you?'

Jerome tells him about the redhead in ski boots and the woman at the newsagent, his teenage sweethearts. He mentions how awkward he feels when he sees them now.

'Sylvie Deshuchères, the newsagent? I'd be surprised,' interrupts the inspector. 'She's not from round here. She and her husband moved to the area fifteen years ago. They used to have a shop in Lille, but had tax problems.'

'Our hearts forever', thinks Jerome. If Sylvie Deshuchères isn't who he thinks she is, who *is* the author of that promise? He'd like to go back to the swimming pool, study the walls in the café, take fingerprints, try to recognise the handwriting. He suddenly believes that the hand that wrote those words would be able to guide and reassure him. He thinks about his wife, about young girls, reviews a succession of faces – which of them has his unfaithful memory *not* betrayed?

'So that's the problem,' Cousinet continues, undeterred. 'They all know each other. They know the family, the gossip. It's too close. Of course, occasionally there's someone new who comes along halfway through school. Pandemonium. Everyone falls in love with the same person at once. And the result? Jealousy, rivalry, revenge, and later: crimes of passion. Clementine Pezzaro arrived in February. Her father was from Le Havre.'

'How do you know?'

'It's my job. Locating people's easier than you think.'

Jerome would like to ask Cousinet to locate Vilno Smith, from whom he's had no news for more than ten days, since the keys, since the rain. He knows she's coped with seven abortions, but doesn't know her telephone number. He suspects that putting a balled fist into the back of her knee might produce a distinctive reaction in her, but doesn't have her address. He's not even sure he knows her name. Vilno Smith. She must have invented it. Names like that don't exist. He struggles with the sheer weight of these uncertainties. He regrets not touching her, even if just in passing, a hand, or a shoulder, just to know what it felt like.

'Hold fire, though!' The inspector is still talking. 'I'm not saying Armand's death is connected to Clementine's disappearance. Absolutely not. You can't let yourself be taken in by timing. Still, wouldn't you like to nip up to the father's old workshop with me? Fabrice Pezzaro's. They lived over the garage, the pair of them, father and daughter—'

'Did you know she was baroque?' Jerome interrupts.

'Baroque? Who do you mean?'

Jerome has got the wrong word. He can tell. It doesn't make any sense, a baroque teenager. But that *is* what Rosy told him. Baroque. He didn't understand immediately and she had to explain it for him: white foundation, black make-up on the eyes and lips, crow-black hair, silver-buckled boots, skinny frame, crosses, coffins, jewellery with skulls and crossbones.

'I don't know,' says Jerome with the unpleasant feeling that he is digging himself in deeper. 'I don't know why I said that.'

'You're still very upset,' Cousinet says soothingly. 'What happened is so sad. So inexplicable. How's Marina?'

'She's gone back to school,' Jerome replies.

The inspector has the good grace to accept this as a reply.

'So, would you like to come up to Pezzaro's old workshop with me?' he asks again after a pause during which he studied Jerome's face. Handsome bone structure, remarkable cheekbones, eyes only just too far apart, a tall forehead, slightly drooping eyelids which give him a tender, penetrating gaze, a long, thin mouth, probably capable of developing the sort of smile he can't resist, almost wider than the face itself.

'I don't know. Yes, why not? It's always good for an estate agent to see where people live. But aren't you meant to be going alone? Isn't there professional secrecy? And what about the warrant? Don't you need a warrant?'

'In films you need a warrant, you're right. But it's very different in real life. You'd be surprised. Go on, say yes – there's so much loneliness.'

Jerome gets the feeling Inspector Cousinet has just made a mistake. He couldn't pinpoint how or why. A feeling of embarrassment creeps over him, but he can't explain it any more than that. He expects the other man to retract or apologise.

Before, he thinks, people didn't talk to me. They didn't see me. And now, it's like I've got some illness, they come over to me, confide in me, tell me such intimate things. Is that an effect of grief? Do the bereaved enjoy a special status? As if, because we've been touched by death, we've temporarily left the usual world, the land of the living. Have I set off across that river without even realising it? It's a distant memory, a history lesson at secondary school, ancient Greece, a ferryman with a very boring name who takes people across the river. He's never forgotten the image because, just as the teacher mentioned it for the first time, Jerome was struck by a powerful sense of déjà vu. What a relief hearing someone talking about something he'd always known, the in-between world, neither living nor dead.

'Yes, that's a good idea, actually,' he eventually replies. 'It'll make a change.'

They order another beer, chat some more and decide to have supper together.

Cousinet does the driving. If one of them has to be breathalysed, it would be better for the old-timer to be the one to take the rap. They travel for forty-five minutes, listening to the radio, and finally reach Vitran-lès-Limons, a village Jerome didn't even know existed, nestled in a recess at the foot of a cliff. The manageress at the inn calls the inspector by his first name; she also says my darling and my pet. Jerome wonders how you go about achieving that sort of trust and intimacy.

'Do call me Alexandre,' the inspector tells him.

By the time they are on dessert, they are like old friends. Jerome laughs and talks too loudly about everything and nothing. He forcibly restrains himself from getting to the point. He can feel himself sliding irresistibly towards the moment when he talks about the forest. He knows he mustn't, that it's too early. Why keep a secret for more than fifty years only to give it up to a stranger after three hours' conversation? From time to time the sentences piece themselves together in his mind: 'I often have to go deep into the forest. I scratch and dig, I need to smell, I run, roll into a ball, lie out flat, resting my cheek against the leaves, stroking the grainy underside of bracken, collecting spores.'

Whatever happens, he must hold back these words, repress them.

In order to deflect these forbidden sentences, he drowns himself in small talk, asking Cousinet for advice about what to wear, what to read. There's no stopping the inspector; he talks about Giorgio Armani and Claudio Magris, Yohji Yamamoto and Yasunari Kawabata. Jerome daren't say that, with all these names, he wouldn't know the writers from the designer brands. He'd like to ask Alexandre how he managed to accumulate such diverse knowledge, and find out from him what courses you have to take to get into the police force. He'd like to be like him.

When they come out of the restaurant they don't get straight into the car. Alexandre takes Jerome by the arm.

'Come, I'm going to show you something,' he says, letting perfect clouds of condensation escape from his lips.

Jerome follows him along a path, then over some stones. The few lights from the village dwindle and fade.

'Don't be frightened,' whispers Alexandre.

Jerome deploys a huge wide smile, invisible in the darkness. He's never afraid in the wild. The further he is from people, the better he feels. The deeper the darkness, the better he can see.

'Look up.'

A shower of stars spills over them. They look so close they seem to be tumbling.

'Close your eyes.'

They take a few steps back.

'Open them.'

All gone. The vault of the skies has darned its every hole and not a single glimmer can filter through. Alexandre holds Jerome's arm more tightly.

'It's funny, isn't it? Someone's eaten all the stars.'

A sob extinguishes itself in Jerome's chest. He isn't fooled. No need for light or a map to work out where they are. Outside but with no sky, protected from the rain but not the cold, in a darkness even deeper than the night itself, your ear drawn by watery murmurings, tricklings, drip-drippings... under the folded wing of a cliff, in a cave as tall as a cathedral's nave, open like a vast ribcage, inhaling the least breath of wind, hungry for air and emptiness, hollow and empty and icy. This is where he fled from – from this cave or one like it, the region's full of them – to find Annette's hand. Some part of him grasped that, if he stayed in the lump of decayed rock any longer, he would have no choice but to turn into an animal. He remembers the temptation: losing language that he had so recently conquered, doing away with thought, hope and sadness, keeping only gratification and fear. Making do with two emotions.

The horror he felt at becoming a simple beast won over the pain of becoming a man. He ran on his little legs, helping himself along with his little arms, propelling himself towards daylight, filthy, bleeding, the animal instinct in him guiding the human that he was to the edge of the forest.

Alexandre moves closer, puts an arm round Jerome's shoulder, breathing heavily.

Oh, right, this man's in love with me, thinks Jerome, amazed not to be amazed by this, thrown by the fact that he gets it, not knowing what to do with this certainty, convinced yet again that doubt is more comfortable by far.

He lets himself be hugged, indifferent, patient. He knows he has it in him to discourage the most passionate enthusiasm. It's a talent of his, one he doesn't use much and which, most of the time, is a disadvantage. Now his steadiness and inertia aren't struggling – with the passive determination so familiar to him – *against* his happiness, but are effortlessly protecting it from a relationship he doesn't want to have.

A few minutes later the two men are back in the car. Snow-flakes the size of feathers have started falling. The windscreen wipers squeak, the headlights bounce blindly off the silver muslin veiling the road. Jerome is driving, too quickly, as usual. Alexandre is keeping himself amused saying all sorts of stupid things inside his head: 'Yes, that's right, go ahead, kill me.' Jerome wonders how he can make him understand that he understands, that there's no point talking, that it's impossible but it doesn't matter. 'Let's stay friends' would be the most all-embracing formula, but it's so overused, so worn. That's the problem with words, thinks Jerome. People talk so much, not to mention television and the papers. Everywhere, endlessly, words, sentences, the same sentences: 'I love you', 'That's great', 'That's life'. Could we, just for a moment, go back to the prehistory of language, to its discovery, its infancy, to a time when every term was deeply rooted in its own origins, trailing them along behind it, when people spoke so little that every utterance produced astonishment?

'I so badly need a friend,' Jerome says in the end.

'And what about me!' Alexandre replies, laughing. 'You are funny, aren't you! No normal straight man would ever say what you've just said. Something that sentimental. I so badly need a friend. No one talks like that.'

Jerome thinks that Vilno Smith talks like that and has contaminated him.

'We need to find a different way of expressing ourselves. It's essential,' he says, with such conviction he himself finds it disconcerting. 'If it carries on like this, we won't be able to say anything to each other any more.'

'Put it there,' offers Alexandre, reaching his left hand out next to the steering wheel.

Jerome puts his right hand in it, very gently. It is a pact so solemn it makes them both tremble.

The following morning, under a blue sky reflected by the snow, they are trudging towards Fabrice Pezzaro's workshop. Two tiny black silhouettes climbing a wide white pillow. They abandoned the car further down for fear of skidding on the hillside. Jerome hasn't slept all night. When he got home the night before, he found Marina in a terrifying rage. As soon as he stepped through the doorway, she launched herself at him, beating him about the shoulders and face, and sending a volley of kicks to his shins.

'You have no right to do that!' she shrieked. 'You have to tell me. You'll always have to tell me now. I'm not normal any more. If you don't come home, then you must be dead. Since Armand, if someone's late, it means they'll never come at all.'

She cried for a long time and Jerome hated himself for not calling her, for forgetting her, for not thinking about death for a few hours.

He could then have gone to sleep beside her, on the living-room sofa, but he had an idea, an idea that took up every bit of space and filled the night with its reverberations. Excitement and impatience started humming through his limbs, and after that there was no question of closing his eyes, nodding his head and slumping. He sat there motionless until seven o'clock in the morning, stroking his daughter's head as it rested on his knee. An idea like a vision, like an arrow.

Taking care not to wake Marina, he took his notebook from his jacket pocket and wrote the word 'enquiry' in capital letters. He read it and re-read it. The story was condensed within it: beginning, middle, end.

I've got a friend in the police, he thought with a smile, and this revelation opened up a wide pathway to everything that had been hidden until now. Alexandre's a sleuth, he doesn't miss a thing, he knows Sylvie Deshuchères's past, he knows everything about us. Nothing can resist him, no appearances can trick him. He's guided by his intuition, and his methods have been tried and tested. Perhaps he would even be able to find the car keys lost in the mire.

After the visit to the piggery, Jerome went to Besançon. He wanted to have a spare key made, but there wasn't a key-cutter in his village. The man he found proved pessimistic. Impossible to make a duplicate of that little scrap of metal.

'But what if I lose this one?' Jerome asked.

'It's tricky,' replied the man, stroking his full beard.

'Which means…? What could be done?'

'Nothing.'

'I wouldn't be able to get into my car? I wouldn't be able to start it?'

'No, you wouldn't.'

'I'd have to abandon it?'

'Yes. Or give it to a breaker's yard. They'd give you a hundred euros for it.'

'For a car worth two thousand?'

The key-cutter shrugged. He was fatalistic.

'You'll just have to hang it round your neck,' he advised.

'What?'

'The key. Wear it like a necklace, like youngsters do.'

Jerome pictured himself wearing his key on his chest, where other people wear a cross or a locket housing a picture of a loved one. Has it come to that? he thought sadly. The idea was unbearable.

'The man's useless,' says Alexandre when Jerome tells him about the escapade as they trek towards Pezzaro's workshop. 'Nothing easier than duplicating keys. I'll do it for you, if you like. At worst, you could always change the barrel. Put a new lock in.'

'But why would he say that? What's in it for him? He'd have done better to have done the work. I'd have paid him.'

'If only it were that simple,' Alexandre sighs, taking a pause from their climb.

He looks at Jerome, his heart bruised by the man's candour. He's never known anyone so helpless.

'Someone...' he starts to say. 'Someone...' he says again.

He is hesitating before carrying on, trying to find the words, reminding himself of the scrupulous precision their recently concluded pact requires of him.

'Someone wants to make us believe that causality dictates everything, that the world's governed by mathematical laws. They want us to think that every act has a traceable motivation; that we, us, humans, are directed towards an identifiable goal. Let's take your example with the key-cutter. He's a tradesman and, in your view, his goal is to make money, so if he tells you your key can't be duplicated, then it must be true. Well, no, it's not. He said it because his reasons were unreasonable, given on a whim, to do himself down, because he's tired, because his wife's dumped him. We don't have a clue really. If it were that straightforward, people like me would be completely redundant. Culprits would wear their crimes written across their foreheads. Do you see?'

'So how do the police do it, then? How do you go about finding out?'

'I search, I scour, I dig. With each new enquiry I forget what I think I know about human nature. Let's say I'm like a jam jar.'

Jerome smiles. Alexandre reels. Just as he thought. A smile he simply can't resist, wider than the face, the picture of childish delight. He pulls himself together, rapidly builds a brick wall to contain his feelings.

'An empty jar,' he clarifies. 'And I fill it up with every tiny thread, crumb and dust particle of the story. When I've finished, when the jar's full, I shake it and the solution appears.'

'Always?'

'No.'

'What do you do if it doesn't appear?'

'I start again.'

'And if it still doesn't?'

Alexandre looks down towards his feet, which are covered in snow and are invisible, as if he and Jerome have taken root in the dense flakes.

'If it doesn't appear, it makes me sad. The pain lasts for a few weeks, a few months and then, one morning, it evaporates. I don't know why. It's a very nice feeling, very luminous. The case that was such a stumbling block stops being a case, it becomes an enigma, or a mystery, if you prefer; and it joins the groundswell of enigmas and mysteries that make up our life: what are we doing here on earth? Who created us? What happens after death?'

Jerome looks up towards the hut at the top of the hill and starts walking again. His legs feel light, his whole body seems to be pumped with helium. He's flying. His chest opens wide, he takes deep, calm breaths. He feels ready for anything, in *astonishingly* good shape. There, he's done it, he's used that word he wanted to use. Even under your breath, even inside your head, it still counts.

From the outside it looks like a hay barn. Walls made of wooden planks painted over with engine oil, corrugated iron roof. It's a tall square building with almost no windows. The double doors in the north-facing gable end are closed with a padlock. Alexandre manages to open it without any trouble. It takes a few seconds. Jerome doesn't see a thing. His attention is drawn to a clump of mistletoe determinedly attacking a pear tree a few metres below them, the dying tree's frail black branches colonised by the opportunist plant's leafy green stems.

Inside there is a stifling blend of smells: damp straw, petrol and rubber. The stale air is just waiting for a match, to go up in flames. Piles of tyres make every dark corner even blacker, deadening everything, quashing any light, trapping the least ray. Moped carcasses, motorbike engines, brake cables, accumulations of spark plugs and heaps of cans lie about, unified by a layer of filth, a greasy black dust that clings elastically. It is difficult to pick a path through these obstacles that clang together making a sound like a cow bell if you so much as touch them. Alexandre's torch produces bluish-white circles on the paler boards of the ceiling, and on the walls. A haphazard slide show invites itself into this halo which moves around as nimbly as a songbird – it is of details from posters stuck to the walls: the Marlboro cowboy's hat, a ship's hull carving through a wave, women's buttocks outlined with lace, huge breasts, naked bottoms, thighs with fingers positioned here and there, half-open mouths crowned with beads of sweat... Alexandre points his torch at Jerome.

'Well?' he asks.

Jerome doesn't know what to say. He tries to avoid the beam.

'Give me your first impression,' Alexandre says, deflecting the torch. 'Without thinking about it. It's important. What does all this say to you? Everything we've just seen.'

Jerome thinks: a man. It says a man. Virility. But he doesn't say that. He doesn't know why he feels so out of place with these images and smells. He's a man too, after all. But coming into this place, it's like... He doesn't have the words to describe the experience, although several come to mind: 'temple', 'lair', 'dump'. The problem is the sentence. Thinking of a sentence. He needs his notebook. He thinks that, if he wrote, he might be able to formulate what he's feeling. The combination of disgust and envy.

'I'll help you,' says Alexandre. 'Could you see yourself living in a place like this?'

Jerome laughs out loud. A generous laugh that starts in his chest and springs freely from his throat, a fountain, a geyser. A laugh that women have often tried to provoke because then, when they do, something very nice happens inside them. Alexandre tightens his grip on the torch, clings to it. Everything hurts, his lips, his stomach, his knees.

'No, no, no,' Jerome replies, still laughing. 'Never in my life. But do you think he slept here?'

'Let's go and see. There's a door at the top of the staircase.'

They climb the wooden steps, making the banister sway as they hold on to it tightly.

On the first floor, a dark, smelly apartment. Passageways leading to troglodyte dens, the damaged landing floors giving under every footstep. Beer cans, plastic bags, a smell of urine and patchouli. One of the rooms is painted entirely in black, the window masked by a curtain of leather, which amuses the two visitors. There are coffins, and these are black too, in various sizes, nailed to the walls or piled up on the carpet, full of pencils, cigarettes, knickers, crucifixes. You could fit a child of four or five in the largest of them, but you'd barely squeeze the corpse of a field mouse in the smallest.

'This is the daughter's room,' says Jerome.

The Goth room, he says to himself, completing the sentence, relieved that the exact term has come back to him at last. Goth like Gothic. So, do Goths venerate death? He senses that he shouldn't elaborate on the subject.

'Looking at this,' Alexandre reckons, 'you'd be inclined to think young Clementine committed suicide. The coffins, the crosses, all this black. But there's actually no connection. Goths don't want to die any more than the rest of us. It's an aesthetic that they find soothing, confining, but it's never more than an aesthetic. Do you see what I mean?'

But it would be so much more straightforward if she *had* committed suicide, thinks Jerome.

'Yes, I see,' he replies. 'But having a father who's a sex maniac could make you want to end it all, couldn't it?'

I love this boy, thinks Alexandre, in love with Jerome's sense of propriety.

'You're getting ahead of yourself,' he tells him. 'When you're investigating, you have to keep deferring the conclusion. Observing, gathering, being sure *not* to analyse. Letting the ideas come, but letting them slip away as well. When you're investigating, it's vital to forget you're hoping to find anything. You have to make a point of dissociating the two. For example, right now I'm forgetting that Clementine's disappeared. I'm forgetting that her father sold Armand a Triumph.'

I'm forgetting that a ring with a skull and crossbones fell out of my shoe, thinks Jerome. But it doesn't work. He can't stop thinking about it, as if the piece of metal had burrowed into the arch of his foot.

'I'm even forgetting Armand's dead,' adds Alexandre. 'I'm forcing myself not to know anything, not to have any of the facts. That's the method I use, the jam-jar method.'

Jerome wants to believe in it and yet, when the inspector says he's forgetting about Clementine's disappearance, the Triumph and Armand's death, it has the reverse effect on him. The more the inspector erases, the more Jerome experiences an irresistible eureka.

'Are you sure they've left?' he asks, feeling increasingly anxious.

He's afraid Alexandre will broaden the scope of his search, will come and dig up the soil in his garden just where the ring came out of the mud.

'The father definitely. He's closed his accounts and gone back to where he came from. That's what most runaways do. It's so painful setting off into the unknown. I've picked up his trail in Le Havre. He's gone back to his old job as a scrap-metal merchant.'

'And the girl?'

'Not there. As if she'd never existed.'

'She might be with her mother,' suggests Jerome, desperately trying to deflect Alexandre's attention. 'She has got a mother, hasn't she?'

He feels a more and more urgent need to keep the inspector away, to substitute one enquiry for the other.

'Why should she have a mother?'

'Everyone has a father and a mother!' Jerome cries, one tone higher than he would like.

'Do you really think that?' Alexandre asks tenderly.

Jerome feels utterly transparent. It's painful, but also a relief for him, given that he never really had a father or mother; sixteen or seventeen years of stand-ins, at the very best. He wonders what else Alexandre knows about him. Perhaps he knows more than I do, he thinks. He now urgently wants to get things straight on the prying the inspector is guilty of.

'What do you know about me?' he roars, with one hand at Alexandre's throat, gripped by an urge to throttle him, to smash his head against the wall, to fall into his arms.

'Nothing,' Alexandre says calmly. 'Nothing more than you've told me. Nothing except what I've seen. A wife catching a train. A daughter crying over her dead boyfriend. A rural estate agency.'

Jerome releases Alexandre's neck and takes a step back. He wants to apologise, to explain that he's never this brutal. It's because of the tyres, he thinks, the tyres and the posters, like a force sleeping inside me that has suddenly woken. He is also aware that this man, who is so gentle with him, provokes him. Alexandre looks at him with… how could he describe it? He looks at him with far too much affection, and it's suffocating. It's thrilling too. With this gaze turned on him, he feels taller, stronger, he feels warm. He'd like to stay there, the way you want to stay in a shaft of sunlight, your body gorged with heat, caressed by the light. But it's uncomfortable and, after a while, exhausting too, because there is nothing beyond that gaze, nothing to be experienced, other than disappointment.

'I was married once,' Alexandre says after a pause.

Jerome has sat down on the edge of a coffin, his knees hugged to his chest.

Here we go, he thinks. The illness is spreading again. Inspector Cousinet's going to tell me all his secrets. And what am *I* going to do when I've got loads of stories to tell? Where will I spill them?

But the question that's really tormenting him is a completely different one. Who will listen to mine? That's what he'd like to know. He's never talked. Paula knows nothing about the time he spent in the bracken. Marina doesn't know her father was a foundling. He feels fake, hollow, riddled with holes, his joints ache and his mouth has gone dry.

'Her name was Eva. We met at a demonstration. She was very left-wing. I was in civvies. She was an incredibly broad-minded woman. I mean, she did marry a homosexual policeman, and that's no mean feat,' he laughs. 'She didn't put it like that. I was something else to her, as if she looked at me from a particularly quirky angle. We used to translate Latin together. Did you do Latin?'

'I was no good at school,' Jerome grumbles.

'Neither was I, but I've always liked Latin. I wasn't as good as Eva. With her, it was her job. But I sometimes found unexpected solutions which really impressed her. She liked making love with her head resting on her Gaffiot.'

'What about you?'

'Me... I didn't like it. I...'

'What's a Gaffiot, anyway?'

'A dictionary.'

The image puts Jerome into a turmoil. Making love on a dictionary, making love with a dictionary.

'It's much more common than people think, women who marry homosexuals,' says Alexandre. 'They find it reassuring. They don't have all that fear of the predatory man. They feel free, they feel strong. And then one day they feel ugly, or old, or lonely, because we don't want them enough, or not at all. They want to feel like someone's prey again. They leave us. Anyway, in my case, I didn't want children.'

'Why not?'

Alexandre doesn't answer. He opens and closes a miniature coffin, clicking his tongue against the roof of his mouth.

'My father was a nasty bastard,' he says eventually.

'What happened to her, your wife?'

'She had three daughters with a dramatist. A playwright. A drunk. At first it was so passionate. Such a gifted Latin scholar! That's what she used to tell me on the phone, and it wasn't difficult to translate. But later, the girls grew up, and the dramatist… She always called him the dramatist, even when she went to see him in prison. She would say, "I'm going to see the dramatist."'

'Why did he go to prison?'

The question goes unanswered. The two men sit in silence. A crow calls, perched on the roof.

'I never knew my parents,' says Jerome, expecting his very skin to rip, his bones to turn to dust under the pressure from these words that have been held back for so long.

'That could be a good thing,' replies Alexandre.

And, because Jerome says nothing, because he tilts his head, shrugs his shoulders and looks overwhelmed, Alexandre thinks he has just made a blunder. How could he say something so stupid?

But it isn't his friend's remark that has Jerome so perplexed. What he finds alarming is how imprecise, how vague his declaration was. He thought he could put an end to his silence with that sentence: 'I never knew my parents.' He often saw it unfurling in his mind's eye, as if on a ribbon at the foot of a coat of arms. He liked saying it to himself. He hoped it would give him instant deliverance. But which parents does he mean, exactly? Who *are* his parents? And when he says he didn't know them, does he regret that he doesn't know the identity of his biological parents or that he knows so little about the couple who raised him? Who would the statement be about?

'I've got a job to offer you,' he says to Alexandre, looking up suddenly.

Before he says it, he doesn't know what's going to come out of his mouth. He talks as a way of understanding. A way of knowing.

'I want you to investigate something for me.'

'What sort of thing?'

'Let's get out of this place.'

Jerome stands up, hurries down the stairs and goes out into the snow, blinded by the sun. He stuffs his hands into his pockets, fists closed. His heart is beating far too fast. His throat is so tight he couldn't get a single word out. Against his left forefinger, he feels the cold metal of his car key. Against his right forefinger, the same contact. Another key. His house key? No. Right pocket or left pocket, the shape's identical. The lost key's been found. He brandishes the two identical keys under Alexandre's nose now as he catches up with him.

'What are those?' Alexandre asks.

'My car keys. In my left hand, the spare. In my right hand, the original!' exclaims Jerome.

'You hadn't lost it after all. The key was at the bottom of your pocket all along.'

Jerome shakes his head.

'No, no,' he says in a dreamy voice.

'It's funny,' says Alexandre. 'It often happens, but we never think of it. We're so busy preparing ourselves for losing the things that matter most that we accept their loss too quickly. Misplaced glasses on a forehead, or the end of a nose, gloves in a handbag. The other day I spent five minutes looking for my mobile, when I had it in my hand. You'd think we'd learn. It's a metaphor for life, don't you think?'

'No. It's not a metaphor,' retorts Jerome, although he's not sure he knows what the word means. 'This key wasn't in my pocket. It is now, but it wasn't yesterday. Someone put it there. Someone slipped this key into my coat pocket.'

'A practical joke?' asks Alexandre.

'A message,' Jerome corrects him. 'Do you know how carrier pigeons know where they're going?'

'Yes.'

'Well, I don't, but this is the same. It's like I've just received a message attached to a pigeon's leg.'

'And is that what you want me to make enquiries into?'

Jerome doesn't answer. He launches himself down the slope with a bounding step. His heart is flooded with joy. Oh, if only these teenagers didn't keep going and dying, he'd be so happy.

8

At the agency he had twelve people to see. Jerome ticked them off: a cross for the couples, a dash for singletons. There's even a star in the middle of the list: daddy, mummy and twin girls. He had to say: hello, goodbye, yes of course, you said it, in the present climate, I can't disguise the fact, in an ideal scenario, a lovely neighbourhood, double-glazed bay windows, particularly in springtime, it's a stretch but so perfect for you, the price?, bearing in mind changing interest rates, don't hesitate to call.

He had to smile, shake hands, stroke heads, lend biros, open out roadmaps, take the phone off the hook, punch figures out on his calculator, furrow his brow, listen, listen and listen. People's lives, the ones who complain and the ones who show off, and never, not even once, someone speaking from the heart.

Jerome wants knees that open wide as a stork's wings, collar bones that emerge from under a lumberjacket, long arms gesticulating around a face. He wants to see the madwoman again. He wants Vilno Smith to come into the agency with her jacket parachuting behind her, and social niceties thrown to the wind. He has now been waiting for her for four hours at the site of their first meeting where, he believes, she arranged to meet him by returning his car key.

Between two clients, he takes out his notebook and writes the words: 'pigeon', 'snow'. His temples are throbbing, the bones of his skull tightening together. He tries again. 'Who are my parents?' 'Annette and Gabriel Dampierre.' On the Internet he tries to find contact details for Mr Coche, the solicitor he went to for his inheritance, over thirty years ago. He finds nothing. Mr Coche must have died, and Jerome doesn't know where the papers are. He imagines that somewhere, on some deeds of sale or a death certificate, there will be a record of the information he doesn't have: a date and place of birth. What has he done with these documents? Where's he shoved his family records book? Paula must have taken it with her. She used to deal with administrative things. It's as if he's erased his own tracks. He has a mental picture of a fox sneaking off with its belly to the snow, its brush – the very word – sweeping the path in its wake.

After he has dealt with Mr and Mrs Grignard, who are selling a plot of grazing land on the edge of the village, he rummages through his files. The boxes of archives soberly lined up on a shelf reveal a worrying lack of order: property details mixed in with Marina's school reports, the menu from a restaurant in Venice, and gas bills. Like a pack of cards shuffled by a professional, there is no logic, no hierarchy. 'I'm disorganised,' he writes in his notebook. 'Disorganised fox,' he puts on the next line.

The telephone rings. Paula's voice seems to be coming from way, way back in the past.

'How are you, big boy?'

'Middling,' he replies. 'It's good to hear your voice.'

'Thanks. I didn't want to disturb you sooner, but… I think about you a lot, you know,' she says in a shaky voice.

'Me too,' he lies.

'How's Marina? She never answers my calls. Never calls back.'

Jerome wonders what he can invent. He doesn't know anything about the state his daughter's in. Marina's anxious, he thinks. I have to warn her if I'm going to be late. She's not normal. She frightens me.

'She's gone back to school,' he replies, as he did the day before, when Alexandre asked.

'But how does she seem in herself? Is she eating?'

Jerome goes shopping twice a week, and makes supper in the evenings. He usually sits down to eat alone. Marina's friends picnic with her in her room. She grabs a cup of coffee in the morning before going to lessons, presents him with her

143

forehead so he can give it a quick kiss, and disappears into the cold, her hands tucked inside her coat sleeves, without a hat or a scarf, and sometimes even with wet hair. He's annoyed with himself for not doing more to protect her, for not scolding her, but how would he go about it? She's become a stranger to him.

How do you deal with your child when childhood is over? he wonders. It used to be so simple: he read her stories, played her music, carried her on his back and went round the house on all fours; they painted together and did puppet shows. Paula thought he was so patient. 'How can you spend so much time playing with a child? I find it deadly boring.' For Jerome, it was the exact opposite. It took no effort on his part. What he found exhausting was the serious world of paperwork, parents' evenings, the mask he felt he had to put on the moment he stepped into his office.

When she reached adolescence, he was afraid his daughter would turn her back on him, would rebel. But the divorce saved them. Paula left. She was the baddy. He and Marina stuck together, went to the cinema, watched debates on television, and sang at the top of their lungs with competitors on talent shows. When she went out for the evening, he told her not to be back too late. If she went past her agreed curfew, he would sulk the next morning. She was an easy child.

But she'd turned into an adult now, all of a sudden, as a result of Armand's accident. What use was he to her right now?

What use are parents to children who've grown up? You can't play any more, or scold. What's left? Funds being transferred from one bank account to another. All that's left is money, and Jerome doesn't have much.

'She's eating. Yes, yes, she's eating well. She doesn't look as if she's lost weight,' he tells Paula as reassuringly as he can.

'Oh, I'm so glad. So she's coping okay?'

Jerome knows why Paula's calling. She's got a new boyfriend and can't bear her own guilty conscience.

'Yes. She's coping really well. She's got so many friends round her. They're a very tight-knit group, lovely kids.'

'That's brilliant. She'll get over it. It's like when she was little. Do you remember? She'd get really high temperatures, but she recovered very quickly. She's tough, our daughter.'

Tough, thinks Jerome.

While listening half-heartedly to Paula, he writes in his notebook: 'She's a Dampierre, a dans-pierre. She's made "in stone". And her mother has a heart of stone.'

'How about you, big boy? How are you? Not too hard, is it?'

'I've got lots of work. The market's picking up. Interest rates are falling, so people are buying and selling. I'm up to my eyeballs, actually.'

'Well, that's great,' says Paula. 'That's really great. It's good to hear your voice.'

'Yours too, my darling, yours too.'

Paula coughs at the other end of the line. She's having trouble swallowing that 'my darling' that he slipped into the conversation out of pure cruelty, to punish her for repeating what he said a few minutes earlier. My darling whose body will always belong to me. What do you do with your darling when she lives a thousand kilometres away, when she left without any explanation and comes back for twenty-four hours in four years to bury a young man she never knew and sleep with her ex-husband just to have something to do? 'My darling,' he writes in his notebook, drawing a flower over the 'i'.

'Right, well, big hugs to you, then. Tell her that Mum thinks about her all the time.'

'I'll tell her.'

He hangs up. 'Mum thinks about you all the time,' he writes.

Isolated words and short sentences are accumulating in his notebook as if to form a poem. Jerome remembers the card he wrote for Annette's birthday when he was eight. He had spent a lot of time trying to find a rhyme for his mother's name. He wanted 'Annette' to rhyme with 'beautiful', and was put out that the best he could manage to make his compliment into anything like a poem was 'pet'. What could he do? He waited a long time for the words to arrange themselves harmoniously, for the beautiful tender feelings he had to be transcribed onto the carefully folded sheet of paper. Not succeeding, he copied out, from memory, the first verse of a poem learnt at school:

The doe wails in the pale moonlight
Weeps till her heart is torn
Her enchanting little fawn
Has vanished in the dusky night

He signed it with his own name and wrote at the top 'For my mummy who I love', surprised that he found it so easy to form the letters of a word he had never been able to say. He read this heading back to himself. The word 'mummy' reverberated inside him. Impossible to say it out loud. When Annette opened out the piece of paper, she cried: 'Oh, my God, my God!' and buried her fist in her mouth as if to stop herself screaming. He was both proud and ashamed of his fraud.

Thinking back to it now, it is – rather oddly – the words 'dusky night' that he finds moving.

I've never visited my parents' grave, he thinks. He doesn't know anything about the rituals surrounding death. No one initiated him into them. Annette and Gabriel had made their funeral arrangements down to the last detail. Jerome didn't have to take care of anything. Everything was recorded in an organised fashion in a book: the choice of funeral directors, the site of the grave, the lease on the burial plot, the prepaid bill.

How do you wake up one day intending to plan your own funeral?

Perhaps they found it easier doing it together, the two of

them, like an excursion. Did they have so little faith in me? Jerome wonders. They left the table, taking the tablecloth with them, and all the crockery's on the floor. There's nothing of our life as a threesome left.

Jerome tries to picture his own death. It doesn't make any sense to him. I'm alive, he says. And he can't get further than that. Banging into the brick wall of life. Unable to see beyond it. I'll never die, he thinks. Until the day when I do actually die.

How did Annette and Gabriel do it? Was it down to illness? Acting as an advance warning? Jerome doesn't think so. They were most likely already dead, he concludes, dazed by the logic of this sophism which is as implacable as it is flawed.

Marina's bag lands on his desk, sending all his paperwork flying. He didn't hear her come in.

'My poppet,' he says, closing his notebook as discreetly as possible. 'My poppet…' he says again.

Marina never comes to his office.

She's seeing me with my mask on, he thinks, rubbing his face vigorously.

'What's…?'

His words tail off of their own accord.

There are great tears rolling down his daughter's face. She stands there wide-eyed in front of him, crying as if that – the sight of her father as an estate agent – is what's upsetting her so much. She's so pretty, with her runny nose and her cheeks red with cold. When she was a baby, Jerome thought she was even sweeter when she cried, her nose all screwed up and her mouth twisted. He was devastated by how expressive that miniature face could be, like a grimacing cameo.

Her eyes are beseeching him, her hands, reddened by the cold, are gripping the desk between them.

'Is it your half day?' he stammers.

Marina shakes her head, her eyes still pinned on him, an adorable gorgon. The outside air came in with her, a smell of moss, lichen and snow. He's never seen this expression on her face before.

When she was crying for Armand, you could see the anger in her eyes; today it's terror.

'I'm pregnant,' she murmurs between sobs.

Whose? With what? How? My little girl? Pregnant? Time stands still then sets off again, at great speed, in reverse, as if knocked back down from the top of a hill. Leaves swirl up from the ground towards the branches, turn red, then green again. Autumns come to die in the heat of summers that barely have time to change into springs before freezing into winter. Clothes shrink, bodies grow smaller, disappearing into nothingness. Marina hasn't been born yet and soon Jerome himself is back inside his mother's womb. A young girl. His mother. A very young girl. Jerome's mother, so little, lost, with no one to talk to about it, no one to help her. The silence, the shame. Hiding.

Giving birth without a sound, in the forest, alone. The child living in a den, feeding him, clothing him, talking to him, a secret wild child. Every day the terror that he might have been eaten, that the rain might have washed him away, the mud swallowed him up, the cold killed him. Willing him to die, a deliverance, an end to the lies, the fear, the exhaustion. Finding him unharmed, weeping with joy, cuddling him and saying, 'My love, my love baby, my baby love,' building him a hut, finding him a cave, hearing him babbling. The infant never cries. He knows what he's up against. He knows he can trust his mother, she is good, she loves him. Very soon he's on solids. Very soon he's on his feet. He never strays too far. He understands perfectly. She would so love to boast about it. My son's a genius, he's strong, he's never ill. He stands so tall on his little feet. He says, 'Mummy.' She says, 'Wait for me, watch the sun and when it goes behind that branch, I'll be back.' He listens and waits and watches the sun. When the sun reaches the branch, she comes back, with an apple or some biscuits. She makes him little figures out of wood. Together, they call them Family: Daddy, Grandpa, Granny, Auntie, Uncle. Together, they count: one, two, three, four. When you get to five, you clap your hands. For three years, the winters are mild, the autumns dry, the springs warm, the summers temperate.

'Someone's watching over us,' she tells him, pointing at the sky.

'Daddy?' he asks, pointing at the moon.

'Daddy,' she replies, 'yes, Daddy's taking care of everything.'

Then one day when the sun drops behind the branch, she doesn't come. He goes to sleep, waits for the next day, and another. Chews on his sticks, the family shredded, bites into berries, curls up in a ball, looks at the sun, lets another day go by, scratches at the earth, groans, counts to himself, waits, looks at the sun. She doesn't come. The animals draw closer, sniff at him, he cries out to frighten them away. He runs, leaving behind his den, his cave. She'll never come back. He lets himself slide down stony slopes, tumbling from the top of a thorny bush, rolling among flints and leaves, and landing on a track. In the distance, two slow, heavy, unfamiliar figures holding hands. Slip his own in theirs. Trotting along on tiptoe, not crying or talking, reaching them, slipping his own in theirs.

'Everything's going to be fine,' he says, getting out of his chair to take his daughter in his arms.

Marina struggles, punching him. He holds her more tightly.

'Listen, my poppet. Everything's going to be fine. I'm here. I'll help you.'

'But it's disgusting!' she cries. 'It's like I slept with a dead boy.'

'No, it isn't, it isn't. Don't say things like that. You're still so young. This has just landed in your lap. You don't know.'

'I know exactly. My life was a fuck-up, and now it's even more of a fuck-up. I'm eighteen, I'm a widow and a single mother. Does it look good to you? A widow and a single mother at eighteen. Do you think that's a good start? It's like I've been through everything already. What's going to happen to me?' she moans.

'We'll take care of this. We'll do whatever we have to.'

'Call a doctor. Call the hospital.'

Marina takes the phone off the hook and hands it to her father.

'Tell them it's an emergency. Ask if they can do it this evening.'

She's screaming. Passers-by, ill-defined in the gathering darkness, peer through the window. Quite a crowd has formed. Seeing the father and daughter fighting, some of the gawpers consider intervening. A few kicks, a few punches. Jerome offers no resistance, lets Marina pummel him. He has no strength. His body is asleep and his mind daydreaming. He's thinking about children that aren't born. He should have been one of them. I'm a survivor, he thinks. My mother offered up her belly to the hooves of an irate foal, tumbled down stone steps, drove knitting needles inside herself, drank potions and poisons, but I wasn't having any of it, I hung on. What a thought. And here I am today, fending off punches... No. *Not* fending off punches from my little girl, my baby who...

'You don't have to keep it,' he tells her, his nose bleeding. 'But you don't have to get rid of it either.'

Marina freezes. Her arms drop by her side. She has stopped

crying. She slumps into the chair with a sigh. Jerome sits at her feet with his back against the desk. He feels so tired. He'd like to go to sleep like this, with the mounting pain from his bruises. He doesn't know the rest of the story. Nothing's happening the way he thought it would. Still, he's got to play out the scene to the end, look up, talk some more, make a decision, do something. Couldn't someone take over here? he wonders. I don't know what I'm supposed to say.

There's a rope strung tightly between now and later, above the chasm, in the dark. The daughter has climbed onto the father's shoulders and, with his arms stretched out for balance, he walks forward. He has to get to the other side, without losing his balance, without dropping his child.

He allows himself to do some sums. The woman who brought me into the world must have been sixteen to eighteen. Let's say seventeen, it sounds right, seventeen. The one who adopted me was forty-seven. Let's get an average, seventeen plus forty-seven divided by two equals thirty-two. A thirty-two-year-old mother is about right, that's how old Paula was when Marina was born.

Jerome doesn't know where these ideas are taking him. He's hoping for refuge in numbers. Numbers which, at first glance, are so soothing – they're intrinsically sensible, rigid, infallible – soon let you down because they get you nowhere, they organise without classifying, regiment without resolving.

He thinks about the baby in his daughter's tummy. It's like a poplar leaf, he tells himself. Green for a moment, silvery the next, at the whim of the wind. Green which is alive, silvery which is not because it implies petrification and immutability. One minute I'm happy, everything is simple and charmed, the next I can see my daughter's life ruined. A poplar leaf, light, round, with its serrated edge, inoffensive, not harming a thing, sifting through updrafts. Expecting a child. Expecting someone you don't know. Well then, why do you expect it? You don't expect it, and along it comes anyway. Or not. Once it's there, it's forever. Armand's parents will be his parents until they themselves die. How could you not be frightened? In a whole lifetime, you don't have many opportunities to impose such a weighty sentence on yourself. You get used to the short-lived, feel comfortable with the intermittent, or repeatable. You'd like to be able to negotiate. If Marina keeps the baby, she will be a mother, that's an absolute. She will be an Absolutely-mother. If she loses it, she won't be an Absolutely-not-mother. Life won't let you put it into equations. There's always a bit left over, a lack of symmetry that flings the whole system apart.

Jerome feels that, if he manages to think straight, he will make it to the other side. But it's impossible. It's on a slope. He's going to fall and take Marina down with him.

He calls Paula back.

'What's the matter, big boy?' she asks.

Marina shakes her head, wags her index finger under her father's nose. She doesn't want him to say it, but he will say it.

'You've got to come. Marina's pregnant.'

After a pause, Paula asks:

'How many weeks? Has she done a test? Let me talk to her.'

Jerome presses the receiver against his daughter's ear as she fights, then accepts it and takes refuge in the office toilets.

Practical common sense, he thinks. There. That's exactly what I haven't got. Paula always asks the right questions. She doesn't lose her head. She knows that the numbers that matter right now have nothing to do with mothers' ages. Mothers' ages – it sounds like some mathematical joke. Whatever next? The numbers that matter are to do with late periods, hormone levels. What does he know about it? Nothing. He can't see how he could ever talk to Marina about that sort of thing.

The whole question of instincts is the only one he keeps asking. He hasn't learnt to live the way other people do, by talking, and thinking. Something in his body is triggered before his brain has a chance to intervene. He is surprised, yet again, to find himself envying animals their silence, their fatalism. Eating, being eaten, giving life, losing it. Animals swish through life, following a perfect trajectory, never hesitating, never giving up, never changing their minds. They don't even know crossroads exist, but are propelled like arrows from the divine bow, with only one mission: to complete the perfect arc, from birth to death, to teem from nothingness back to nothingness, gracefully and weightlessly. By comparison, human destinies strike him as so tortuous, so clumsy, heavy and compromised.

The gaping onlookers through the window have dispersed. All that remains is a tall figure protected from the cold by a lumberjacket. She raises her hand, about to knock on the glass. Jerome drops his head and rests it on his crossed arms. He doesn't see Vilno Smith putting her hand in her pocket and going back the way she came, melting into the darkness, surrounded by silent snow that has started falling again.

9

Jerome is looking through the window at the white garden. The metal table is topped with a perfect cylinder of snow. The two chair seats are covered with fluffy cushions. Forty centimetres fell in a few hours. At the far end of the garden, near the small doorway onto the road, a black stalk pokes through the cocooning layer, brandishing a tufted grey seed head. Everything else is covered, hidden, protected. What *is* that plant? Jerome wonders. How dare it break up the uniform innocence of the view? Even the rowan and the elder have had the good taste to take on globs of snow that have turned them into great frozen flowers. A dandelion? Impossible, too bendy, the stalk would have bowed. Cow parsley, perhaps, with just the dried-out skeleton left. Cow parsley, he says again for his own benefit. Vilno Smith's favourite.

He looks at it for so long that the garden shrinks until it is reduced to a single luminous, intangible point. The past. Memory. It's the same, Jerome thinks. The same feeling, exactly.

An inaccessible beauty; just looking at it kills it. Touching it destroys everything. But there's joy all the same, and hope, an almost mystical impulse.

I remember. A sentence tracing its way, so swiftly. It shoots onwards, heading down, boring on unhindered, the heart's going to give way, you think, it's too wonderful, too rewarding. The speed is suddenly frightening, it's going to shatter everything. There will be nothing left.

Two blue tits in a clinch tumble from the sky which is as white as the ground. The two pairs of wings beat through the air. The couple twirls for a moment before disappearing into the cylinder of snow. A few flakes fly away and then the birds re-emerge with their fragile heads, their delicate bodies, their claws as fine as a child's eyelashes, and there they are playing, rolling in the snow and scattering it all over the place.

'Marina! Marina, look at this!'

But Marina isn't there. Jerome knows that. He called her without a sound, inside his head, in memory of the good old days. She would have so loved watching the blue tits' ballet.

The birds disappear, swallowed up by the sky, and Jerome looks at the now spoiled garden. The insignificant destruction. The end of perfection. Children do that. Love does that. Makes a mess.

It's a long time since Jerome has been on his own. He can't remember how you deal with your roving thoughts, with the time. For all those years, even when there was no one at home, even when he ran away to the forest, he wasn't alone; Paula would be waiting for him, Marina would soon be back from school. When his daughter went away to see her mother, he could count the days, knew he was on borrowed time, started preparing for her return the minute she stepped out of the door.

'Jerome?' a voice calls behind him.

He doesn't answer, doesn't move.

'Can I come in?'

It isn't locked. Rosy need only turn the handle.

Jerome hasn't looked round to watch the young Manchurian shake off the snow that has gathered on her coat and her hair. He hopes she won't see him either. But that's stupid because he's by the living-room window, opposite the front door. And yet he feels so flimsy, so feeble, he thinks he's disappeared.

'Jerome?' Rosy calls again in her lilting voice.

A minute earlier he could have treated her to the sight of the blue tits, but he has nothing to offer her now. Why won't she give up? What does she want from him?

He hears her heading for the kitchen, recognises the clink of the cafetière, the rustle of a pack of coffee, water running from the tap.

A few minutes later the smell spreads through the house. Tears well in his eyes. Gratitude, sorrow, joy, regret? Jerome doesn't know.

Two cups have been put on the waxed tablecloth. They have been filled. A teaspoon is turning.

'I came by because, well, it seems a shame to stop seeing each other, doesn't it? I kind of got used to it and…'

Jerome turns round, very slowly, like a rusty weather vane driven by the lightest breeze.

Rosy looks at him, appalled.

'Oh, my God, you look horrendous! You look like you've lost half your bodyweight!'

The exaggeration makes Jerome smile. He grinds his teeth. He comes and sits across the table from Rosy. She pushes his cup towards him, puts two sugars into it, stirs it for him.

'That's kind,' he murmurs, surprised to hear his own voice.

Rosy shakes her head. Her cheeks blaze.

'In your family,' she says, eyes lowered, 'you all think I'm kind. Marina used to say it the whole time too. But at home they think I'm a pain. My parents can't stand me. My mum, my dad, both of them. They can't agree on anything, except me. My dad calls me "the lump".'

'Oh, he doesn't,' Jerome manages, almost automatically.

'Oh, but he does. Do you know why? Because I don't do anything they want me to. I eat too much. My parents are thin. They think I'm disgusting. I've always been fat.'

Jerome wishes he could tell her otherwise, say she isn't fat, but it's undeniable. He wishes he could say it doesn't matter at all, that she's lovely just the way she is, like a Manchurian pony.

'Parents...' he sighs.

He can't work out where to go from there. Parents get everything wrong, he thinks.

'It's because of me,' Rosy says, her cheeks still scarlet, glancing up briefly.

Jerome doesn't understand what she means.

'It was me who put the idea into Marina's head,' she ploughs on.

'What are you talking about, my little songbird?'

Rosy cries. No one has ever called her 'my songbird'. A great hulking albatross, that's what she is. A monster.

'You're the most adorable girl I know,' Jerome announces, even though it takes a lot out of him, even though he's not used to making this sort of declaration.

Rosy looks up, her mouth tiny in her huge face.

'I told Marina about my vision. The business with the graveyard and the boy carrying her bag.'

'So?'

'Everyone knows I've got a gift as a medium,' Rosy explains solemnly. 'All my friends know. I sense things. Even if you don't believe in it, it's true. You know the fire at school three years ago? I predicted it. And the priest who ran away with the fire chief the day Magali Graton got married, I predicted that too. I've always been like that. I've always known.'

'What's the connection?'

'It's because of me that Marina thought she was pregnant. It's because of me she's left.'

Rosy breaks down and sobs. Jerome drinks his coffee, lulled by Rosy's tears.

Marina believed she was expecting a child. She's gone to be with her mother. Paula said she would take care of everything and that's what she's done. She took her daughter to the doctor, who explained that the emotional shock had disrupted her hormones, and everything would settle back down.

'Poor darling,' Paula said to Jerome. 'She hadn't even done a test. But I could see straight away she wasn't pregnant. A mother can tell things like that. For now, I think it would be better if she stayed here. I'll sign her up to do her schoolwork by correspondence. She's going to get some rest. The doctor said she needed a change, a change of scenery. At your house, everything reminds her... Well, you get the picture. Here she's seeing new people, thinking about other things. It's better for everyone. How about you, big boy, how are you feeling?'

I'm feeling awful, Jerome thought. I'm feeling abandoned. I'm feeling like a marathon runner who has victory snatched away on the home straight. I'm feeling like a man who'd gladly kill the mother of his child because she's never done anything for her and has snatched her away from her father so easily, with one phone call.

'It wasn't because of you,' he tells Rosy, taking her chubby babyish hand in his. 'This goes much further than that.'

'But do you believe in my gift as a medium?' Rosy asks, dry-eyed.

'Why not?' Jerome shrugs.

'Because my parents don't believe in it. My mum says I've made the whole thing up. She says I'm just trying to get attention, because I'm so ugly I'll never find a man.'

Jerome lets go of her hand.

'That doesn't make any sense.'

Now it is Rosy's turn to shrug.

'My mum can have any man she wants.'

Jerome thinks about Rosy's mother. She runs a hairdressing salon in a small street behind the church. She changes her hair colour so often that he struggles to recognise her from one time to the next, but her buttocks don't change, her breasts, her waist – a perky body, vigorous, available. She already had that reputation back in high school. At thirteen, everyone knew she'd done it. She married a bicycle salesman, a sporty type with a low forehead, gleaming biceps and a militant hunting, shooting and fishing mentality. Jerome came across him once in the forest in his cycling gear. He was hugging the trunk of a hornbeam, then suddenly stepped away from it, made a sign of the cross and said 'Amen' three times before hugging it again. Jerome didn't want to disturb him. He slipped silently into a ditch out of sight and couldn't wait to forget.

'D'you know, I never knew my parents,' he tells Rosy.

'Did they die when you were little?'

'I don't know.'

Rosy frowns.

'I was abandoned. I lived in the forest. And then, one day, a lady and gentleman found me. They were called Annette and Gabriel, and they brought me up.'

'So you knew them. *They* were your parents.'

'No, I didn't know them either.'

'You know, Jerome, that's a very big secret,' Rosy declares admiringly. 'Because I never suspected a thing. I never guessed. And it's really nice hearing a story you don't already know. That's the first new story I've heard.'

'That's because you can see the future, but not the past,' suggests Jerome.

Rosy shakes her head vigorously.

'I can see the past, the present and the future. I can see everything. Your particular story's a very big secret,' she says again.

And Jerome feels honoured, as if he has been given a medal.

'I've never told Marina what I've just told you. I should have done. But I never have.'

'I don't believe in the spoken word,' Rosy announces adamantly.

Jerome admires her conviction. He doesn't believe in it either, but he still wouldn't dare state the fact. He feels as if something doesn't quite ring true in conversations. He couldn't put it any more precisely than that. He is often frustrated by, and almost always afraid of, the thought of expressing himself, and is always sure he won't be understood. He blames words, the inaccuracy of vocabulary. It wouldn't occur to him to question the whole system.

'People hear what they want to hear,' Rosy goes on. 'It's no use talking to them. They can just as easily hear what you're not telling them. We talk out of habit, because otherwise we'd just get too bored, but it doesn't change much. Take school, for example. In reception, the teacher teaches children to read. She talks about letters all day, consonants, vowels, all that stuff. And at the end of the year, some of her pupils still don't know how to read. They heard what the others heard, they listened, but it didn't work. Their minds didn't open.'

Jerome looks at her, perplexed.

'With me,' she continues, 'my mind's very open. Too open, actually. It's like a deformity. I receive every wavelength, even the ones not meant for me. And that's why I'm a medium. I told you I could see into the past, the present and the future, and that's true. The weirdest thing of all is reading the present, because everyone should be able to do that. But they can't. Most people don't see anything. If I wanted to make money, I could become a private detective, for divorces and stuff like that. I know who's sleeping with who. I know where, I know when.'

'Are you interested in that?'

'Not at all. It weighs me down.'

Jerome would like to ask her something about Vilno Smith. She's likely to know her. She's likely to know where she lives and how to find her. But why ask her, when she can probably read his thoughts? He might as well wait till she brings up the subject herself.

'Did you know Armand was going to die?' he asks, although he hadn't decided to.

The words were ahead of his thoughts.

Rosy looks away, bites her lips. She waits a few seconds and says:

'I knew he shouldn't have bought the motorbike.'

'Do you know who sold it to him?'

'Well, *you* know. So why do you ask?' Rosy takes a cigarette from her bag, lights it and starts smoking, dragging hard on the filter as if wanting to swallow it. 'Did your friend ask you to question me, then?'

'Which friend?'

'Inspector Cousinet. What a stupid name. He's the one who wants to know. What difference does it make to him? No one's pressed charges.'

'He's got a theory,' Jerome counters.

Rosy nods her head as if this answer has satisfied her. She drinks her coffee. Takes a powder compact from her bag and brings the mirror up to her eyes.

'Do you think mascara looks any good on me?' She lowers the compact and moves her face up to Jerome's, pointing at her lashes, and opening her eyes wide. 'Does it bring out my eyes?'

Yes, thinks Jerome. Your lovely eyes, your eyes like a cow's, a donkey's, your gentle Manchurian pony's eyes, they're as warm and black as coffee. He takes a sugar lump between his fingers and rolls it into the palm of his hand.

'I don't know much about make-up, you know, my chicken. I'm just a dad. I don't know anything about that sort of thing.'

'Oh, what the hell do I care! What fucking difference does it make!' she snaps fiercely, picking up her bag. Her body undulates inside her clinging black clothes. She clears the cups in silence, then washes them up.

Jerome has hurt her, she won't come back now. He'll be on his own. The house will always be empty now. No daughter, no gang of friends, no beer bottle tops left under the dining-room table, no leftover tobacco by the sink. Not a single voice, a single laugh. He's old, he's alone, it's over.

Rosy sways down the corridor, takes her coat off the peg, without a backward glance at him. He needs to say something to stop her leaving, to make amends. She puts her hand on the door handle.

'Rosy,' he calls.

She doesn't turn round.

'Look at this.'

He rushes to the window and opens it, the birds have come back, they're fluffing themselves up, sending snowflakes flying like feathers.

The door slams in the draught. A gust of wind blows through the house. Jerome leans over the balcony and throws the sugar lump he has kept in his hand into the garden. The cube of white crystals disappears in the snow, leaving no trace, the tiny pit immediately sealed over, collapsing in on itself. That's how I'll go, he thinks to himself.

10

It's the fourth time Alexandre has taken a train in five days. On the platform at the Gare de Lyon, he's pleased with himself for packing so well. A small compact suitcase fitted with wheels stands next to his leg. Slung across one shoulder, he has a camera bag with his various tickets stowed in an easily accessible outside pocket. You don't lose them, he thinks, you don't lose skills like that overnight.

The preliminary meeting with Jerome took no more than a quarter of an hour. Alexandre knows the ruses for extracting crucial details while the person being questioned isn't aware of revealing them.

Sometimes a name is enough.

It was the only time Jerome smiled, that he seemed to relax.

'My mother's maiden name? You'll like this. It's almost a joke, like it was predestined. Landau. Annette Landau. The word means pram, for goodness' sake! For a woman who takes in a lost child!'

Alexandre carried on with his questions quite neutrally so that Jerome didn't become too wary. It's important to keep the client completely in the dark until the day you can reveal all.

Other questions followed, about jobs, standard of living, friends and acquaintances. The two men worked together to root out old proofs of address and obsolete tax slips. All they found were the letters Jerome had sent his parents when he was at holiday camp. Small sheets of paper folded in four and crammed with untidy writing, the words shifting between different levels within one sentence, like notes in a stave – the melody held in his words. Jerome put the date in the top right-hand corner and his name in the top left, as if it were a piece of schoolwork. He uses the expression 'I'm having quite a nice time', which catches in Alexandre's throat. At one point there's mention of a 'mean camp supervisor', and Alexandre can't help asking:

'Why mean? What did he do to you?'

'I can't remember.'

Jerome also tells his parents that he has bought them 'a little surprise' with his pocket money. It brought tears to Alexandre's eyes. Love has that effect on him, it always has. He melts.

'There's nothing about them, you see?' Jerome said when they had finished their search. 'As if they burnt everything.'

'Perhaps they did,' replied Alexandre.

'What do you mean by that?'

'Nothing. I just know that some people don't want to keep any trace of the past.'

'What sort of people?'

'There are no rules.'

During the first phase of his enquiry, at the Paris Historical Library in the Marais quarter, Alexandre came across a lot of tourists. He told several of them how to get to where they were going. This is where he lived for four years with his wife, Eva. She paid almost nothing for a rented garret room with electricity but no water. Every morning they carried pitchers up the tortuous staircase, leaving a constellation of dark droplets on the treads. They shared the toilets with twin sisters, Louise and Marie-Louise, suffragettes in their nineties who were as skittish as young goats. The neighbourhood was nothing like what it has become now. There was a constant hum of sewing machines, rubbish accumulated along the pavements, the buildings were blackened with coal smoke, and gangs of youths confronted each other endlessly. Alexandre hadn't been back since then, and he savoured its familiar crossroads, felt indignant about renovations, thought about stretches of road that had vanished, replaced by luxury boutiques and café terraces full of men watching him.

He secretly thanked Jerome for sending him on this pilgrimage.

As soon as he heard his friend's mother's maiden name, he knew he would be going back to his old stamping ground and couldn't wait to pack his bags, as if invited to retrace his own beginnings.

'I'd like to see the file on a foreigner who was naturalised just before or just after the war,' he said at the library reception.

He is simply applying his so-called jam-jar technique. The only scrap he has gleaned: a name, and, all around it, nothing, silence. A string of letters dancing in a vacuum. The lack of clues can sometimes be more significant, more powerful than an accumulation of details. A life apparently swallowed up by a black hole. Everything absorbed, light, sound, matter. Only the identity remains.

Alexandre thinks about his research, the excitement of the hunt, the joy of discovery and its direct counterpart, shattering reality and horrifying truth. Enquiries rarely culminate in good news. He who digs should not expect to unearth treasure. Deep down, right at the bottom, there is always filth, decay, envy and cruelty; proof that evil reigns, that crime is accessible to everyone and a taste for destruction lies in every human heart. What am I actually looking for? he wonders. Haven't I had enough? Isn't it time I reached a conclusion, accepted that brother will turn on brother? What a waste, all that time spent thinking, only to end up with a dictum that popular wisdom has been trotting out for thousands of years. What's the point in finding excuses for Cain or aggravating circumstances for Abel? How can I hope to uncover some other motive, better than the one that is so hackneyed it's become grotesque – the Grim Reaper, the skull and crossbones? There's nothing beyond that, and what do we learn once we've put the puzzle together? What do we learn that we didn't already know?

As he asked for the file on this naturalisation, Alexandre felt a familiar fear sweep through him. A bland smell, a cheap perfume, always the same one, however sharp his sense of smell may be – the humdrum reek of death.

A young woman whose eyes focused resolutely in opposite directions advised him to consult her colleague at the National Archives Research Centre on the rue des Quatre-Fils.

A blue sky punctuated by white clouds was reflected with great precision by each puddle. The pavements felt narrower than they used to be. The buildings were too pale, as if they had been scoured, sending a golden sideways glow onto the faces of passers-by.

At the Archives Centre he found the reference number for the decree that corresponded with Annette Landau's naturalisation. Unlike Jerome, he knows how to work out where a name comes from. That's a remembered skill too, he thought, lying to himself, because this had nothing to do with experience, but involved heredity, or rather inheritance.

It was his father's speciality: identifying foreign names,

truncated patronymics: 'So take Monsieur Dembin, for example, at the hardware shop,' he would tell his little boy. 'Well, that's Dembinski. See how it works?'

Inspector Cousinet senior had a pretty high opinion of his teaching skills. He liked riddles and puzzles and crosswords. Alexandre thought these games boring and preferred drawing shapes (scribblings, in his father's view), pathways coloured onto pages that he tore from old newspapers with shrill names like *Le Cri du peuple de Paris* or *Le Pays Libre*. That was how his mind developed, in the loops and contours that, before he could even read, he traced around words whose leaded ink stained his fingers. He felt that when he tracked these pastel-coloured meanders with his blackened index finger, he would achieve a different sort of reading, one that was both more allusive and more profound.

Armed with the decree's reference number, he would now have access to the naturalisation file, but for that he had to leave Paris.

During the second phase of his enquiry, at the Centre for Contemporary Archives in Fontainebleau, Alexandre mostly came across students.

Grey-faced and self-important, they smoked three cigarettes in quick succession during their rare breaks, loitering at the foot of the French flag which flew from the top of a pole by the front door. He recognised them as soon as he was on the

174

train, and his intuition was confirmed in the shuttle bus. They were suffering from getting up too early, and had nothing but a cup of bad coffee inside them. These novices hadn't thought to bring a sandwich, and they regretted it once they reached the inhospitable site whose ugliness was in direct proportion to the splendour of the former mansions he had visited the previous day. Alexandre finds it amusing that contemporary archives should be kept in a place so devoid of charm, as if its architecture were conveying a message about recent history: 'Beauty ends here, don't go hoping for anything.'

In the room set aside for people to consult records, he ended up opposite an Asian researcher in her fifties. Her black hair was divided by a streak of white which perfectly captured the square of neon positioned just above her head. From time to time she tipped her wide face backwards, as if sunbathing in the cool blue halo directed at her. She closed her eyes and took a deep breath.

He was tempted to imitate her, but, worried she might take it badly, settled for sliding his white wooden chair over the spotless floor tiles. A slight backward movement before consulting the naturalisation file for Annette Landau, widow of Abramowicz.

There it was in the very first lines, beneath the date 22 July 1953: Annette had been married before the war. Her husband had died in a death camp. Alexandre photographed the document.

Further on, he learnt that Annette spent the last two years of the war in captivity, in a work camp in Switzerland.

He could have stopped there. Told Jerome that his mother was a foreigner, an Eastern European Jew, and that her first husband was murdered by the Nazis. But one question drove him on: how had Jerome managed to avoid knowing? How had the foundling succeeded in maintaining his ignorance? There was probably some secret, some truth buried away. But for how much longer?

Alexandre re-read the file and felt it was so concise it was almost suspect, as if the portrait had been simplified, an outline drawn in bold strokes, omitting even the most superficial details. Instinct or skill? He couldn't tell which on this occasion; either way, he was quite sure there was something he wasn't getting.

Hiding the truth requires more intense effort than most people realise; it takes concentration and constant restraint. If Jerome never knew any of this, then someone had made sure he didn't know, and if someone had made sure he didn't know, then it was because they felt the truth was intolerable. It's the myth of the happy idiot, of ignorance as a guaranteed shortcut to happiness. Someone protected him because they loved him. Someone felt it was better for him to be stupid than unhappy. Alexandre was touched by this concern, but experience had taught him that, in the end, things turn around and you eventually suffer the unhappiness of being stupid.

He now had to find the report for the arrest, go a little further back in time, and for that he had to travel again, all the way to Switzerland.

The small sum Jerome had given him would not cover the expense of this last journey, but he was happy to give it to him as a gift.

At the outset he meant to refuse any financial transaction.

'I'm getting my pension now. This is an extra, for the pleasure of it.'

But Jerome had insisted.

'It's better if I pay. I could look into this myself, but...'

'It would take you forever. People who aren't used to doing it panic. They don't know where to start.'

'No, it's not that. As soon as I try to concentrate on this, and I start remembering, and I try to understand what's missing, I feel like I'm on the edge of a cliff. My legs go all shaky and I can't see anything in my mind's eye. Everything goes blank. The more I concentrate, the more it all vanishes.'

'It's a pleasure for me to help you.'

'I must pay for this.'

Having found his seat on board the train to Switzerland, Alexandre is studying a map of Bern. First, he locates the

Martha guest house where he has booked a room, then he puts a red dot on the opened-out map to mark the site of the canton's confederal archives. If time allows, he'll make the trip by bicycle. He opens his notebook and writes down his guest house's address and telephone number, then the details of the research centre. He thinks about this other aspect of his technique: writing everything down. That comes from his father too. Writing and re-reading.

In his notebooks, Inspector Cousinet senior referred to himself in the third person: 'Cousinet hiding out at the Zanzi, on the rue Neuve-des-Cloîtres, orders a beer, goes down to the toilets to get on the blower. Pays for his tipple...' Alexandre could hear his tenor voice with its rough-hewn accent the moment he opened one of the hundred black books with red spines that he hadn't succeeded in getting rid of when his father died.

Then one day he burnt them, all of them, in a clearing in the Rambouillet forest. It was a Tuesday, at dawn. Three hours to burn ten kilos of paper. A treasure going up in smoke, he thought, as he watched the incandescent pages glow for a long time before turning black and disintegrating to ashes. He could have entrusted them to a museum: a museum of policemen, of informers, of failed writers?

He goes back to the early pages of his own notebook, where he wrote the account of Armand's funeral. There is a sketch of the cemetery with figures around the coffin. With the help of tiny arrows, he has identified the key characters: the father, a huge man, his right shoulder topped with a circle – a bird had settled there, he remembers; a ball of feathers fluffed up in the cold. The mother, smaller, narrower, her head bearing a chignon too heavy for her; and, close by, the brothers. Standing stones, a family of standing stones. Facing them, another figure has a five-pointed star above it. He recognises Jerome. Remembers the first time he laid eyes on him. My type, he thought, already resigned. His type: naïve, awkward, helpless, a mummy's boy who steals every woman's heart. Above Paula's head he drew an asterisk, and over Marina's a simple cross.

He had first heard about the accident from the local newspaper. It was barely two months after Clementine Pezzaro disappeared. Youngsters missing from the roll-call, having fallen into some ravine, some river, some lake, some ditch; lives stopped just as they were starting – he's never been able to bear it. He went to the funeral to see, to understand. He stared at the gaggle of teenagers, blessing them just in case, praying they would be spared. Their eyes were red, their jaws slack, their feet turned inwards, their knees bent together, their backs stooped, their hands going blue. They all looked at the hole, horrified. Just one girl, with Aztec features, looked from left to right with her slanting black eyes, as if on the alert. Her darting agate-coloured irises contrasted with her solid, placid body. She's thinking, Alexandre told himself. She's trying to understand too. Either that or she knows. Her fine eyebrows, high up on her forehead, quivered from time to time as if an electric shock were running through them. She looked at every face, seemed to be looking for someone missing in the crowd. 'Restrained ceremony. Muttering. No religious service. Grandmother singing. Disruption among onlookers. Angry dispersal of some of the cortege. Father's speech in Italian. A good sort,' he reads.

Alexandre closes his notebook, strokes the black cover, lets his index finger slide down the red spine. He thinks about Annette Landau, born in 1910 in Lodz, Poland, came to Paris aged eleven, qualified with a diploma in accounting at sixteen, factory girl in the rag trade until she married Meyer Abramowicz in 1929. She was granted French nationality following her ninth application in 1953, the first dating back to 1925.

From an envelope, he takes a photograph Jerome has given him. Annette must be between fifty and sixty. Her hair is very short and entirely white, her skin olive. She is looking at the lens, with a cigarette in the corner of her mouth, her eyes screwed up because of the sunlight. She almost seems to be winking at the photographer. Her face is thin and very lined, but her shoulders are rounded and her breasts full. The image stops at the waist. She is wearing a brightly coloured blouse with several buttons undone, and round her neck, an amber necklace with beads the size of pebbles. Alexandre puts the snap on the fold-down table fixed to the seat in front of him. He has always thought portraits should be put away when the original model dies. How can we accept looking at a face that no longer exists? It's unbearably cruel, but more importantly, it's false. Unlike painted faces, trapped by the approximations of a paintbrush, faces in photographs are still disturbingly alive, deceptively physical.

Alexandre slips the photograph into his notebook and goes to sleep with his hands crossed over its cover, as if taking part in some spiritualist exercise.

The manageress of the Martha guest house is surly. She flicks the form he has to fill in across the counter and refuses to speak French even though a small sign in front of her announces trilingual capacities: German / French / Italian.

'Are you Martha?' Alexandre asks in English.

She shakes her head.

'My name Sofia,' she replies laconically, not looking at him.

'Who's Martha, then?' he ventures, in the hope of softening her up.

'Nobody.'

He doesn't press the point and goes up to his room, which is under the eaves. The ceiling is so low that he can touch it with the tips of his fingers, and the bed so narrow that it could be mistaken for a child's. He sits down with his feet resting on his suitcase, letting the mud on the soles of his shoes dirty the dark fabric. *What am I doing here?* he asks himself with his head in his hands, wounded by the hotelier's hostility, by exhaustion from the journey, by loneliness and the absurdity of his research. *A few months ago I didn't know this man existed,* he thinks, *and here I am in Switzerland, at my own expense, trying to find out about his mother's life. What's that all about?*

It is nine o'clock at night. The guest house doesn't serve an evening meal. He ate his last biscuit on the train. *I'm being punished now,* he thinks. *In bed with no supper.* He is soothed by the gentle force of habit, the familiar sense of melancholy. He lies down on the small mattress, catapulted back to his silent, reclusive childhood. He strains his ears, hoping to catch the squeak of a door hinge, the creak of a floorboard. In vain. A two-note siren wails in a nearby street. *I'm so far away,* he thinks, closing his eyes to the landscapes flitting past the windows of all the trains he has taken.

Are you Jewish?

    Yes.

    Why have you crossed the border illegally?

    Because I'm Jewish. We can't stay in France, it's very dangerous for us, you do know that, don't you?

Do you have family in Switzerland?

No.

Who helped you?

My cousin.

Did he get you over the border?

No.

Who got you over?

A woman. A woman dressed as a man. She was wearing a peaked cap and speaking a foreign language. A language I don't speak. Not French or German or Polish or Russian.

Was she alone?

Yes.

And you?

No. There were lots of us.

How many?

I don't know. Eight, maybe twelve. There were two children too.

With their parents?

No, on their own.

Are you married?

Yes.

Where's your husband?

I don't know.

Do you have any children?

Yes.

How many?

Four.

Where are they?

I don't know.

When did you last see them?

Several weeks ago.

Where?

We got through to unoccupied France together, all six of us. We had the name of someone in a village near Bergerac. As soon as we were safe I went back up to Paris to help my sister to join us. She's had polio. Her walking's not good. She's got a little boy. But I didn't find them at home. A neighbour told me they'd left. I asked if they'd been taken away by the police. She didn't answer, just slammed the door. They were taken by the police, then, weren't they? So I went back to the Dordogne, but when I got there, they'd all gone. The locals told me some people in hiding had been denounced. My husband and children must have gone further south. I tracked down my cousin and he told me it was too dangerous now, that I had to get out of the country. I wanted to stay, for the children, but my cousin persuaded me. He told me a living mother, even far away, was better than a dead one nearby.

So we left. We walked at night. I don't know the names of the places we went through. At one point it got colder and there was a lot of climbing; my legs hurt.

At the border, we met up with some other people. Jews. My cousin gave an envelope to the woman dressed as a man.

What was in the envelope?

I don't know. I don't think it was money. I can't think what else it could have been. That was when I said goodbye to my cousin. He stayed in France.

Is your cousin in the Resistance?

We're all in the resistance. We're all resisting.

Every time he has to turn a page, Alexandre photographs it. He focuses very carefully and frames it as tightly as possible. His nose is running. His tears fall onto the report for the arrest of Annette Abramowicz, née Landau, drawn up by the Swiss police on 11 April 1943.

11

Jerome is toying with his twin car keys on the counter of the bar at the Bar des Sports. One in each hand like puppets, he walks them towards each other till they meet, then draws them apart. He is only obscurely aware of what he is doing. It is only when Bruno the manager stares at his fingers that he realises how ridiculous this performance is. He smiles, grasps the two sets of keys together and puts them in his pocket with an 'I nearly lost them!' as if that explains everything. The manager thinks he's talking about the keys, when Jerome actually means one of the keys and Vilno Smith. There are good sides to misunderstandings after all. Jerome basks in the sense of peace peculiar to paradoxical admissions, those that cost nothing because the element of truth in them remains hidden. He imagines a world in which everyone talks like that, protecting culprits and victims in a thick screen of pronouns.

Jerome is drinking. He isn't used to spirits. Bruno gave him the choice of two whiskies; he chose the one with the black label.

'You'll see her again, that daughter of yours,' the manager says kindly. 'Our kids'll all be gone one day, anyway. What d'you expect them to do with themselves here? Mathias'll be the same. Once he's passed his baccalaureate – even if he doesn't, actually.'

Jerome gulps down his whisky, orders another.

'That's right, make the most of it,' says Bruno. 'Go on, the next one's on the house.'

This is nice, thinks Jerome, the warmth, the booze, the fatherly solidarity. When we can't cope with what we're meant to be coping with, he remembers. Yes, that's what Rosy said. That's exactly it – I can't cope with what I'm meant to be coping with. I'd have to hang on to the happy bits and bury the horror.

The happy bits. Vilno Smith knocking on the door at the agency. She waits for him to come and open it.

'Can I come in?'

Such grace. Such a face.

'Have you forgotten me?'

'No, I didn't have your number…'

'Blah-blah-blah. It's easy to find people if you look.'

'Thanks for the key.'

'You're welcome. I always give back what I take, eventually.'

'Would you like to see the house again?'

'No. It's you I want to see again. Give me your hand.'

The palm of her hand is against his and it feels as if he's put his fingers everywhere, round the back of her neck, against the arch of her foot, between her thighs, on her breasts, over her armpits, at the back of her knee.

The horror. The following day. Nightfall, tinted blue. A forgotten mildness breathing down from the sky. His skin was grateful to the air for not stinging. His whole body surrendered to a feeling of gratitude, respite. Jerome was strolling round his melting garden dirtied by the thaw. He wanted to pick the tall stalk with its absurd pom pom. The impudent cow parsley that had broken through the carpet of snow exactly where Armand had planted his flower bed. Then, just for the pleasure of it, because there was nothing better to do, he started to scratch at the soil. Softly at first, making the most of its supple texture, which was almost liquid in places; but soon feverishly, like a dog, like a pig, delving into it with his elbows and face, without a sound, holding back his moans, his heart thumping in his temples, his mouth aching. With his expert fingers, he felt some fragments; not as sharp as flint, less crumbly than limestone, not as soft as wood, not as stringy as roots. And, a bit further on, in the corner, the chill of metal. He stalled for a moment before bringing up his findings. He caught his breath.

Bones covered in mud, and a silver cross.

Alexandre left the Confederal Archives early in the afternoon and has gone back to his room at the Martha guest house – a room which, although tiny, does offer Internet access at a price. He knows that if you want the number of a convoy sent to the death camps, the thing to do is to key in the victims' full names on the Holocaust Memorial website. He has always been horrified by how simple the process is. He remembers the day when, having discovered that this database existed, he tested the system, randomly using the name 'Joseph Klein' as his open sesame, where he might have used 'John Smith' in other circumstances. But there are no other circumstances. He felt party to the whole ignominy when, with all the clinical detachment of technology, the machine responded to his typed request, revealing the date and place of death of a real person. He would willingly have done without this loss of innocence, which would have raised a quiet chuckle from his father but left him with a lingering feeling of disgust. Exactly what had he been playing at?

As he sits on his bed, his frozen fingers have typed several spelling mistakes – tactile Freudian slips that briefly keep the dead alive. 'No matches' comes the reply, and Alexandre breathes again. But he ploughs on, types in other names, spelt correctly this time, and the long rectangular window with its grey edge and sky-blue-and-white background appears irrefutably on the screen. Local records office number, then the number of the convoy, where it left from, date of birth, birthplace, and finally, confirmation that the name appears on the 'Wall of Names'.

Meyer Abramowicz has a different number from his children. Alexandre can't understand why they were deported without their father. The enigma hits him like a brick wall, perhaps because of its apparent lack of logic in a system saturated with the stuff. He'd like to know how they were separated. But what difference does it make? When Annette was arrested in Switzerland, her husband was already dead and her children on their way to Auschwitz. She knew nothing. She thought they were safe, somewhere in the south. Alexandre wishes he could protect her, could make sure she never finds out. He wishes he could kill her. But the Swiss had other plans for her. She was brave, strong, in good health. She could work. She survived.

As he writes the children's names in his notebook, a new wave of sorrow comes crashing down over the first.

When he was thirty and bored with routine, he went on a course run by Patrick Fontier, a peculiar young man introduced to him by his ex-wife. Fontier was a spy. He made no secret of the fact. He would admit it after fifteen minutes' conversation, with a slight smile which gave whoever he was talking to every right not to believe him. People thought he was a fantasist. Alexandre had worked out that this was a good way of being left in peace because people so lacked curiosity and tended to trust nothing but the norm. Alexandre had a passion for exceptions. He called the man.

'I don't work with the police,' Fontier told him amicably.

'Good choice,' Alexandre acknowledged. 'I wish I could say as much myself.'

Fontier laughed, and they went on to meet in a café near Nation.

'I want to learn to see things differently,' the young inspector said.

'That's a thought.'

Fontier soon discovered his pupil's talent for deciphering. Sequences of numbers or letters spontaneously revealed their secrets to him. He worked with the help of colours, marking out random pastel-coloured meanderings with a patience and gravity that most people lose at the age of five.

The two men got along well, spoke little, and had a lot of

fun. Alexandre was just about to follow in Fontier's footsteps when he came across his first missing-teenager case, and was reminded of his vocation.

He continued to use what he had learnt from his friend. He had Fontier to thank for his nuanced understanding of motive, concentrating not so much on the common and often misleading question of the grounds for a crime, as on its purpose. By looking at this bigger picture, this grand scheme, a whole new kind of understanding opened up to him.

With his feet on his suitcase, he looks through his notebook and reads back over the names of Annette's children. The four children she had before Jerome, the ones she gave birth to and brought up till they were eleven, nine, eight and four years old, the ones who were starved, stripped, gassed and burnt. His vision blurs, distorting the letters, melting them, putting them in a different order. It is so obvious that Alexandre's throat constricts. His work – is it desecration or long-awaited burial? How can anyone know? – is not done.

Vilno Smith has straw in her hair, crowning her with gold. Her tall body lies full length in the blue moonlight. She doesn't give a damn about the cold. She doesn't give a damn about anything. She sings to herself, stroking her lover's head as it rests on her stomach. Jerome touches her knees, places grains of wheat on her thighs. They make love in the loft of the piggery by day, by night, all the time. Sometimes Vilno brings a bottle of chilled white wine and says, 'Schnapps?' as she hands him a glass. Jerome drinks. He falls asleep, wakes up freezing, goes off to work, runs all the way to his car, never really warms up. In his jacket, between his notebook and his heart, three small bones and a cross like relics.

'What are these?' asks Vilno, having filched them while he slept.

It's time Alexandre left Bern.

At the reception desk of the Martha guest house, Sofia asks, in her elliptical English, whether he would like her to book him a taxi for the station. He doesn't answer, he's looking at her, softened by the faint freckles on the tip of her pointed nose. Behind her, hanging on the wall in a wooden frame, is a black-and-white photograph of a woman. Is that Martha? he wonders. She is staring at him, a note of reproach in her eyebrows.

A few days earlier he went back to his research late at night on a laptop as smooth and black as a tombstone. He waited till sleep had nearly crept over him before checking his intuition. He keyed the name 'Dampierre' into the search engine. Within seconds the result he dreaded appeared, revealing the names of the two children Jerome's father had had before the war. His hypothesis was confirmed.

The pain hasn't left him since. He hides his hands in his

pockets, can't look at his fingers without disgust. He is ashamed of finding out, of understanding.

He has been walking the city's streets aimlessly for more than a week, sitting down in brasseries, watching passers-by, scrutinising faces, expressions, gestures. He sees them alive, imagines them dead. He's been eating badly and the lack of nourishment is exhilarating, digging ruts through his stomach and his mind, producing visions. He's been counting and recounting the money he has left, exhausting himself with subtractions.

'You want me call taxi?' Sofia asks again.

Alexandre shakes his head. He'll walk all the way to the station, dragging his small wheeled suitcase full of stories that have nothing to do with him but that, for now, belong to him alone.

15

'You thief!' says Jerome.

'No, not a thief,' Vilno corrects him, 'a researcher. You won't talk, so I'll pry. It's only fair.'

'The way things are, what difference can it make?'

'You have quite an effect on me,' she continues matter-of-factly. 'The minute you touch me, bang! You just have to look at me and bang! But you're just a country yokel.'

'That's tautological.'

'What does tautological mean?'

'It means a phrase has something redundant in it, like me. Yokel means someone from the country. And country means from the country. It's the same. You're saying the same thing twice. A towny yokel doesn't exist.'

'Who gives a fig! Why do you talk like that?'

'Like what?'

'You talk weirdly, for a country yokel.'

'You're the one who talks weirdly, because you're English.'

'Scottish.'

'Same thing.'

'No it isn't.'

'It's the same to me.'

'Because you're just a country yokel.'

'That's right.'

She's playing jacks with the relics.

'Tell me what it is,' she pleads. 'I love macabre stories.'

'You'll be in your element.'

Jerome takes her to his house, shows her the little garden, the doorway, and where the flower bed is. They go back to the living room to look at the photo album. He gets annoyed because he can't find any recent pictures of Marina. Vilno doesn't say that she saw her at the agency, that she admired her vigorous knuckles and laughed at the sight of Jerome battered by her blows. He is telling her about Clementine.

'I can't see the connection between all these things,' Vilno says very softly.

'It's Armand. It was my daughter's boyfriend who killed Clementine Pezzaro,' he blurts. 'When I got home on the day you stole my car keys, I came in from the back street. My foot sank into the soil, like quicksand. When I took off my wet clothes, I heard a tinkling noise on the floor tiles. It was a ring with a skull and crossbones which had got stuck in my shoe. The girl who disappeared wore that sort of jewellery. They were her bones I found. Armand planted flowers over the grave of the girl he killed.'

Vilno opens her eyes wide.

'Cousinet told me it was the girl's father who sold Armand his motorbike,' Jerome ploughs on. 'Old Pezzaro avenged his daughter. He tampered with the killer's bike. That's why he withdrew his charges, because he'd taken the law into his own hands.'

'But why did the boy kill the girl?' asks Vilno.

'I haven't a clue. Maybe they had something going and she threatened to tell Marina.'

'Do people kill for that here?'

'It doesn't matter. I've managed to distract the inspector, but it won't last long. He'll be back.'

'And then what? Everyone's dead now. It's even. No one cares.'

'What about Marina? If she finds out, her world will fall apart. He was her first love.'

Vilno roars with laughter.

'You're such a romantic,' she says.

'What if she was an accomplice? If Alexandre finds out, he'll want to question her. He's obsessed with these incidents involving teenagers. He'll want to go poking his nose everywhere.'

'Who's Alexandre?'

'One and the same.'

'One and the same what?'

'Alexandre, Cousinet, the inspector, it's the same person. He's investigating Clementine Pezzaro's disappearance. At the moment he's taking a break because I asked him to try and find some information about my parents, but that won't take long.'

'Why about your parents?'

Jerome looks at Vilno. Her wide golden eyes, her short tousled hair, her wilful chin, her madwoman's expression. A foreigner, he thinks. A stranger. She doesn't know anything about me. She wants to know me, but she'll never know me. There's no point making love. Bodies don't say a word.

'But why did Armand bury her at your place?' she probes further, fiddling with the bones.

Jerome is disconcerted by this question.

'Why, what difference does it make?'

'All the difference. It would make all the difference. Or none at all. A boy loves a girl, sleeps with someone else, she threatens to talk, he kills her. Why not? Personally, I don't think it hangs together. But okay, if it makes you happy, let's assume that's all true. Then, once he's killed the girl, he comes and buries her in his girlfriend's garden? It doesn't work.'

'How do you know?'

'I've read lots of detective stories. It's a national pastime in my country.'

'What about the flowers, then?'

'A present.'

'What do you mean, a present?'

'To tell your daughter he loves her. Nothing unusual about that.'

'And the ring.'

'A mystery.'

Vilno says nothing for a moment, thinks, then cries:

'Bingo! I've got it. The father killed his daughter. And he buried her at your place to make people think Armand was guilty. *That* works.'

Two young people have died, thinks Jerome, and here we are lost in pointless conjecture. I'm living in a world where there's not enough fear. Evil is there somewhere, everywhere, and we just laugh, without a care in the world, immoral, blissfully unaware of danger. Such innocence! The word itself hurts him, although he doesn't know why, like a fishbone stuck across his throat.

I'll have to kill her, he thinks, looking at Vilno. Then I'll have to kill Alexandre, and perhaps then I'll be able to rest easy. The whole thing will be just a bad dream, I'll just have to tell myself none of it ever happened – the plan is so simple he finds it intoxicating. And, to finish with, I'll kill myself. A crime with no witnesses – the project is so perfect he finds it seductive. Then he thinks of old Pezzaro and of Rosy. To do the job well, they'd have to go too – a good spring clean is so exhilarating.

In the forest, a shoot of bracken imperceptibly unfurls its fingers dotted with spores. It is slow and silent, no one sees it, not one spectator to watch this performance, and yet it does happen. Jerome feels quite giddy thinking about everything that happens without anyone knowing, all those truths never even noticed. He abandons his planned massacre, rests his head on Vilno's knees and inhales the consoling smell of her thighs.

'You're suffering,' she says, leaning over him. 'You're really suffering. That's what you've got that other people don't have. That's why I love you.'

16

Someone's got to write this story, thinks Alexandre, sitting by his fireplace with his feet on the hearth, which is brimming over with ash. He came home to a cold, empty house. A smell of mouldy lemons has spread round it, despite the temperature. The dust that has settled in his absence taunts him. Someone's got to write it, he reiterates, notebook on knee and pen between his teeth. It will be brief; he wishes it could be longer. He only has shadowy figures, and needs characters. He only knows the broad strokes, when the truth lies in the detail.

He hasn't had anything to eat or drink for over twenty-four hours. His head is twice its usual weight, his eyes keep closing without his even realising, he wakes with a start because of a nagging pain in his neck. Sometimes he dreams, a very short, dense dream, sturdy as an eye tooth. He opens his eyes wide, horrified. His pen has fallen on the carpet. He doesn't pick it up. Goes back to sleep, but not properly. He sees his mother stepping backwards towards the fence around their garden.

She's looking at them, him and his father, on the doorstep. Alexandre's head barely reaches Inspector Cousinet senior's hip. His mother twists her ankles in her high-heeled shoes. She's wearing a lot of lipstick. She steps further away, very slowly. She fumbles behind her, trying to find the gate. She's afraid they'll catch up with her, one or other of them. But neither the father nor the son moves. Alexandre thinks his mother's ashamed. He also thinks she's frightened and he thinks she's right to be. His father's dangerous. *He* is staying, he has to, because he's only little, because inside the house is his bed and under the bed a cuddly toy cat called Moomoo. He frowns. He wants to call 'Mummy!' or to say 'Goodbye, pretty lady', but he can't speak, his teeth are too tightly clenched, his mouth too small. He wakes up again, rubs his eyes. The notebook falls onto the carpet, next to the pen.

17

'It's the month of the rowan tree,' announces Vilno. 'The days are just beginning to get longer, the birds are eating the berries, and the dead go back to their graves.'

She has just got up and her voice is still husky. She opens the window to greet the protector-tree. Jerome watches this woman – who never feels the cold – as she leans out, naked, into the icy air. In the middle of her back, just below her shoulder blades, her spine is visible. You can count each little bone. A game Jerome never tires of. She turns round and smiles.

'The dead stop haunting us,' she says. 'It's a legend, but it's true. In my country, they always plant rowans next to graves because they have special powers. They ward off evil spirits. Do you believe that here?'

Jerome doesn't answer. He can't believe the sun has come back. He thought he'd never see it again. He can't believe Vilno is there, every morning, bitching about French tea ('gnat's piss', she calls it), that she's stopped asking him questions, that she stays with him on his endless walks and can teach him the names of more plants, when he thought he knew them all.

'That's your problem, here in France. You don't believe anything. Santa Claus, at a pinch, when you're little, but after that: banned! The voice of reason. You have to be rational. You plant rowans to attract the birds, and you don't even know they're protecting you, you don't say thank you. Not ever.'

'Thank you,' Jerome says solemnly, just about up on one elbow. 'Thank you, rowan tree.'

'There, that's good. That's better,' says Vilno, coming back to bed without closing the window. 'I'm going to have to move out.'

No, thinks Jerome. Not this. I couldn't cope with anyone else leaving.

'Your daughter will be home for the holidays. You haven't seen her since Christmas. You need to take care of her. I'm just making way.'

Jerome buries his head in Vilno's arms. Her fine dry skin has captured the tentative smell of the wintry garden.

'But I'll come back,' she adds.

Time goes by, thinks Jerome. And nothing happens. He gets letters from Marina, peculiarly starchy ones, as if from another era. She calls him 'my dear father' and tells him about her schoolwork, her grades, her newfound passion for history.

He's impressed by the musicality of her sentences, their perfect balance, the precise tempo, the concise restraint of her descriptions. 'My hair's very long,' she says at the bottom of the latest letter. 'You won't recognise me.'

Time passes and no new catastrophe has descended on him. He realises he is tense with anticipation, a sort of tragic apprehension. There's a corpse in his garden and nothing's happening. Dust to dust. The flowers will be all the more beautiful next year.

Torn pages from the notebook are strewn in front of the fireplace. Alexandre is curled up on himself in their midst. He rubs his cheek, soothed by the rasp of stubble on his palm. He looks sideways at the capital letters he has traced over in red on the pages he tore out.

With one hand he gathers them together, mixes them up, scatters them. Jerome is the sum of six subtractions. Take away six and add one. The only child handed back to widowed parents, to multiply-bereaved parents, the wild child offered up by the forest that had hidden so many.

Alexandre doesn't want anything now. He has it, his motive, his purpose. He thought that beauty would atone for the loss. He was wrong. All the dots are joined and not a glimmer of relief.

He feels crushed by the love of Jerome's parents as if by a waterfall, an avalanche. A mouse nibbles on his shoelace, making little squeaks of delight.

Vilno likes walking through this little town. She likes the word the French use for this kind of place: *bled*. And even though she's a foreigner, she knows it's not a French word. *Bled* is Arabic, it's the wind loaded with sand, the dry heat draping itself over people. But it's also this place, the damp persistent cold, white skies, characterless houses with roofs that are too wide, too heavy, bearing down on the walls and giving most of the buildings a stubborn look. It's the church with its cracked bell-tower, its long scar of plaster, the Bar des Sports with its Christmas decorations that don't come down till April, the exhibition of finger painting by the nursery school children in the town hall. The roads are wider than they are where she comes from. They don't have the strip of moss down the middle that she is used to. The gardens are obsessive – circles dug out round the base of apple trees, beds of petunias under windows, rows of dahlias in front of hedges; or the opposite, terribly unkempt – paint pots piled up on a torn tarpaulin, bits of wood leaning against the skeleton of a mowing machine, paintbrushes, three-legged chairs, broken spades, faded children's toys, inner tubes, bottles, wheel-less bicycles.

This *bled* is ugly, she thinks. And in this ugly *bled*, I found a man.

She is walking quickly, which is normal for her, and with her jacket open because she likes feeling the cold on her skin, being gripped by the air.

The danger is growing by the day, with each passing hour that makes her a little more fond of Jerome. She thinks about the bones, the silver cross, the ring with the skull and cross-bones, the incriminating items that they hid together.

'It's nothing,' she told him. 'It's over now. We can stop thinking about it.'

But that's not true. They act as if they've stopped, both of them, because they want to carry on enjoying life for a bit, to make the most of this inopportunely reawakened appetite, buy the piggery, do it up, make it theirs.

She wasn't expecting to meet anyone.

When, four years ago, her son went off to university in England, the surprise devastated her. She waved her hand bravely on the station platform, then ran to her car with her last smile for Sam still on her lips. There was no strength in her hands, they couldn't get the key into the ignition, were too heavy to put on the steering wheel. She looked at herself in the rear-view mirror, as if seeing her face for the first time in twenty years. How could she be so wrinkled? And where had the sparkle in her eyes gone? What should she do now? No more meals to make, no more anecdotes to listen to, advice to give, permission to grant. She would never have thought motherhood would fill up so much space in her life. Bringing up a child hadn't taken anything. It was easy. She never even thought about it. She liked having to change his entire wardrobe so frequently. Her son grew quickly. His trousers were always too short, so were the sleeves on his jumpers. She was a lenient mother, rarely anxious, never watching the clock, and often out herself. She had sometimes felt pained when she watched other women her age who were so devoted to their offspring, so tautly braced over their homework, so dependent – that was the word that systematically came to mind – on their little ones' successes and disappointments. They're going to be so sad, she used to think, when their young fly the nest. They'll feel so useless, lost and lonely. She felt she was looking down on them. But, contrary to all expectations, there in the station car park, she had joined the battalion of housewives made compulsorily redundant when their children left.

She looked at her hands (which were neither dried out by bleach nor scored by kitchen knives), her hands which were only slightly brown from working in the fresh air in the garden, and suddenly felt she'd been jettisoned to the outer limits of the universe, pulverised by a centrifugal force whose violence she would never have suspected. She wasn't used to feeling sentimental, even less so to complaining. She gritted her teeth, ashamed of falling into the trap, ashamed of her weakness and pointlessness. It would be best just to disappear.

To France, why not? Paris to start with, because it was obvious and she had lived there for nine years from when she was eighteen, instead of going to university, instead of getting married, doing little waitressing jobs, giving language lessons, sleeping with her bosses, her customers, her pupils, never tiring of it, never making anything of herself, but hoping she might grasp some fundamental truth that kept slipping through her fingers. Who was she? Who were they? And what about the world? Were we supposed to find a meaning to it? She found no answers, until the day Lester Gordon came into her life. He was an exquisitely indifferent man whose favourite expression was 'Never mind' and whom she followed back to his native Norfolk to marry him. 'Never mind, it doesn't matter' was the definitive answer, a stop to all questions. How soothing. Alongside the button salesman, she could finally keep her mouth buttoned. It lasted ten years. One as a twosome, nine as a threesome. Then, one day, at Green Park station, a stranger put his fist in the back of her knee. She left, taking Sam with her. Vilno Gordon became Vilno Smith again. That was when time started speeding up, the years piled into each other in a carefree whirlwind, an infernal merry-go-round which eventually hurled her to the furthest reaches of humanity, to the amorphous fringe where childless women go about their business, with no love life and no particular talent.

She chose this *bled* because of *The Flint Year*, the book she mentioned to Jerome the first time they met. She took three trains and a bus to get here. Her cases are still in a left-luggage store at the station in Lille. They can stay there. She doesn't need anything.

She went into the agency when she stepped off the bus because she's always loathed hotels, and although this was not what she told Jerome, she had the funds to buy something. She sat down facing him and, without her really realising it, something gave way. Her ligaments melted on the spot. Her knees suddenly spread, as if her body were deprived of its fundamental tone. She put her chin in her hands and her elbows on the desk because otherwise she would have tipped over backwards. It's physical, she tells herself, when she tries to understand what happened to her. The slope of the eyes, the colour of the skin, the angle of the eyebrows, the position of the nose, the outline of the lips. Sometimes a face bowls you over. Just looking at it is both painful and a consolation. She doesn't remember feeling such a jolt before, can't find the words to describe the exact nature of the impact.

After that, there was the visit to the piggery, her stealing the key, the lonely nights in the cabin, her rushing to hide in the loft when Jerome came back for his car, her comings and goings on the outskirts of the village – buying everything at the discount supermarket where she was less likely to bump into him, eating sliced bread with its toothless spongy texture and cheese spread that went solid in the cold, waiting, doing a bit of spying, dreaming about him, giving the key back, waiting some more.

'Are you following me?' Vilno asks.

'Yes,' says a girl with velvety cheeks, lots of eye make-up and a body like a demijohn.

'Why?'

Rosy doesn't answer. She looks at Vilno, at the lines around the corners of her mouth, under her eyes, on her forehead. She's waiting for a smile to break.

'What do you want?'

Rosy shrugs. She waits a little longer. The smile appears.

'Can we talk?'

'Yes,' says Vilno, 'we can talk.'

Rosy asks her to follow. She walks quickly. Vilno admires the undulations that this girl's body makes in the fading light. As if the brisk rhythm of her walk were superimposed with another more languorous rhythm set to a different tempo.

They walk through streets with improbable names: Lost-Lilac Alley, Horn-Break Way, Lean-at-the-Ready Passage. Vilno struggles to read the signs, despite the growing darkness, as if it were some sort of treasure hunt.

Rosy opens a door, presses a light switch, and throws her coat on the floor.

'This is my house. My mum's at the shop. My dad's at the café. Please, sit down.'

Vilno obeys, pulls a chair up to the kitchen table, which is covered in a waxed cloth with a firework pattern. It's a cramped room with just one window, adorned with curtains in salmon pink organdie with gold fringing. All around her, on even the smallest shelves, the tiniest ledges, are accumulations of knick-knacks: marble Buddhas, spun-glass fish, china shepherdesses, novelty salt cellars, artificial flowers.

'Don't worry about the décor,' Rosy advises, noticing Vilno looking. 'My mother's mad.'

'I'm Vilno,' says Vilno.

'I know,' says Rosy, shaking the hand she is offered. 'And I'm Rosy.'

'Do you know me?'

'Yes. No.'

'Is it yes or no?'

'Both. I know who you are, but I don't know you.'

'And who am I?' Vilno asks, amused.

'You're with Marina's dad.'

'Is she a friend of yours?'

'She's my best friend.'

Vilno nods, touched by the obsolete expression. Best friend. When you're young, it's so important, so solemn, having a best friend.

Rosy makes some coffee, lights a cigarette, wipes her nose, takes out some cups, a sugar bowl, some spoons, cuts a chocolate bar in four and arranges the pieces on a plate, then sits down very graciously opposite Vilno.

'I'm scared,' she says, grinding out her cigarette.

Me too, thinks Vilno without a word. Never show animals you're frightened, ditto with children. Never give in, never tremble. Under the table she clasps her hands together.

'Has Jerome said anything about me?'

Vilno thinks she can hear a coquettish note in this question and is unsure how to answer.

'He may have told you I'm a medium. You're new, but everyone here knows I am. The whole village knows. Something's not right,' she says. 'Something's out of joint.'

Vilno wonders whether Rosy has read *Hamlet*.

'Too many people have died at once.'

'Who's died?' asks Vilno.

'Armand and Clementine.'

'Who's Clementine?'

'She was a girl in our class, a Goth. Do you know what that is?'

'I'm Scottish. We invented Goths.'

Rosy looks impressed and says nothing for a moment before continuing.

'It's not like they died because they were ill. Armand died in an accident, and Clementine, no one knows, she disappeared. That's why I'm scared.'

'Why?'

'It was Clementine's dad who sold Armand his bike.'

'So?'

'So he tampered with the bike so Armand would have an accident. And if he did that, then it was because he wanted revenge.'

'Did he sell it before or after?'

'Before or after what?'

'Did he sell the bike before or after his daughter disappeared?'

Rosy thinks for a moment, looks up at the ceiling, closes her eyes, opens them again and says:

'Before.'

Vilno smacks her hand down on the table, satisfied.

'Well, there you are!' she exclaims. 'People rarely avenge crimes before they've even been committed.'

'I never thought of that,' says Rosy. 'So everything's fine, then?'

'Everything's fine,' Vilno reiterates.

In Achnasheen, the tiny Highland village where she was born, people used to tell lots of morbid stories for entertainment through the interminable winters. They were all false, but they were still bandied about for the sheer pleasure of feeling the hairs rise on your forearms. Those long nights had made Vilno into a paradoxical sceptic. She believed in Druid tales, in the protective power of trees and in elves, but she refused to swallow the fact that Giles had sliced off Tom's hand or that Calum had throttled Fenella. She's even amazed she gave any credit at all to Jerome's theories. Nothing about this story has ever hung together. She should have realised that right from the start.

'But there is something,' Rosy starts again, frowning. 'There's something dark in that house. I've always felt it. Can you feel it?'

That's exactly why I'm drawn to it, Vilno could say, but she shakes her head.

'Maybe it was premonition,' says Rosy.

'Maybe,' says Vilno.

'You don't know anything, do you?'

'No. Are you disappointed?'

'You're sleeping with him, but you don't know who he is. You don't even know his daughter. You're a foreigner.'

Vilno shrugs. What could she say in reply? Everything Rosy has said is true.

'Are we going to get like that too?' the girl asks. 'Are we going to get like you? I can see what's going on. Adults don't have time. They see each other, but they don't know each other. Even when they're married. Even when they have children together. With us, we know each other because we hang out. Because we spend a lot of time doing nothing, stuck together. Because we go to the toilet together, because we drink from the same glass and swap clothes. I don't want to be like you. It makes me shudder just to think of it. Later in life, I'm going to be on my own because adults are all on their own, and that scares me too.'

Vilno doesn't want to lie to Rosy, to tell her that she's wrong and that the more time passes, the closer you get to other people.

'You can't ask life to be like this or like that,' she tells her. 'Sometimes it's good, sometimes bad and sometimes even worse. But childhood stays with us. Time is like a ball. Childhood's in the middle; we're just spinning round it. We don't lose it. I'm fifty. That's old. But inside my head I'm three years old, and eight and fourteen.'

'My mother's not like that. My mother was never eight.'

'You'll be different.'

Rosy's face lights up.

'I *am* different.'

'What was Armand like?'

'He was good looking. To die for. I'm not sure that's come out sounding right, but he was to die for. He was good too. That doesn't sound right at all. It sounds ridiculous, but it's true. You didn't know him so you won't believe me, because if I describe him like that it sounds like a fairy tale. What happened is sad for everyone. I don't know how Marina's going to manage to live now. I've never had a boyfriend. Do you think I'll die like that? Having never been in love, I mean, all that, you know? Marina's way ahead. Do you believe in being good?'

Rosy stops talking abruptly and glances at her watch without waiting for an answer.

'My mum'll be home soon. I don't want her to see you.'

The girl hands Vilno her jacket and shows her to the door.

Vilno wishes she could tell Rosy not to worry about it, to stop being scared, but no words come to her, so she takes those great Manchurian cheeks in her hands and lays a kiss between those quivering brows.

20

The last glimmers of daylight filter into the living room. Alexandre and Jerome are sitting facing each other. On a table, between them, sit the relics.

'I can't do this,' says Jerome. 'I'm picking my daughter up from the station in an hour. I don't know what to do with this stuff,' he adds, pointing at the cross, the ring and the bones.

'Is this what you called me about?' asks Alexandre.

Jerome says nothing. He wishes he could have held out, not told anyone, shouldered the crime, borne the mystery, respected the danger. It's beyond him. With him, the tiniest drop of water is enough to make the bowl overflow, as if saturation were his default state. Yet I feel so empty, he thinks.

'I don't want her to know,' he manages eventually. 'We're going to protect her, you and I. Would you do that? It's your job, isn't it, protecting citizens? Protect my daughter.'

'From what?'

'From the truth.'

Alexandre picks up a bone, feels it, studies it.

'Can we put the lights on?'

'It's what you've been looking for all along, isn't it?' Jerome asks. 'Teenagers who disappear. Your theory, all that.'

He laughs nervously and switches the light on. Alexandre carries on with his scrutiny.

'She wasn't that far away, you see,' says Jerome. 'In my garden, under a flower bed. What do we do? What do I have to do to stop you calling the police?'

'Nothing.'

Alexandre puts the bone down, takes his notebook from his pocket, leafs through it.

Jerome is thinking about his own little book, abandoned God knows where, the hopeless sentences he wrote in it, and the screen that comes up between him and his words the minute he picks up a pen.

The two men eye each other in silence. Misunderstanding looms between them, the confusion driving them apart.

'These bones,' announces Alexandre, laying his notebook on the table next to the relics, 'these bones are old. No flesh. Dry, almost crumbly. I'm not even sure they're human. A long time ago, before you bought your house, some child buried his dog at the bottom of the garden. That just about sums it up.'

'And Clementine?'

'Ah, Clementine.' Alexandre repeats her name dreamily.

'Such a pretty name. Such a funny business. She's reappeared, would you believe it? It's very rare. A former colleague of mine who was transferred to the Vaucluse region called me the other day to say he'd tracked her down. She sells apples in markets. A Clementine selling apples… He had trouble recognising her at first because she's seriously changed her look. She dresses up like a farmer's wife now. It was just a boring case of running away. She's eighteen, her father can't do anything to make her come back.'

'Why didn't you tell me?'

'I didn't know you were interested. I forgot. I had other more important things to tell you.'

Jerome waits for a feeling of relief, but nothing comes; his heart still feels heavy as a stone in his chest.

'And the jewellery?' he asks.

'They're pretty common items. You find all sorts of things when you start digging. Bits of crockery, phials, door handles, keys. You wouldn't believe what people bury.'

Jerome feels foolish. He played cops and robbers, succumbed to rumour, supposition and hearsay. In his search for the truth, he got caught up in the web of distrust that so ably cocoons locals frozen with boredom. He tried to understand, but without following Alexandre's advice, in too much of a hurry to establish connections and reach conclusions, frustrated though he was by the disturbing way the truth kept wavering. Everything had to tally, the disparate pieces of the puzzle had to end up making a picture. What was he looking for? Why did he have this urgent need to resolve things? If I'd written everything down in my notebook, he thinks, it wouldn't have come to this, I would have achieved a degree of patience.

'So?' he says to Alexandre. 'What is it you've got to tell me that's so important?'

Jerome doesn't expect anything. He'd like to feel some curiosity, makes an effort to, but doesn't succeed. He feels the same as when Armand died – dispossessed, detached from his mind, hovering just above and slightly to one side of himself.

I've been doing some digging too, thinks Alexandre. Somewhere else, further away, through piles of paper, virtual entrails. And now I'm going to have to give you this handful of dust.

He takes the picture of Annette from his notebook and hands it to Jerome.

The son stares at the mother, disorientated. He had forgotten another investigation was going on. He is tempted to interrupt Alexandre; wants to tell him that whole business was just a distraction.

Know more about his parents, what for? There would always be a missing link, because behind the enigma of his adoption was the one of his birth. And, having grown up in the woods, he would never know his family tree. The irony of it makes him smile.

'You told me your mother's name was Landau,' Alexandre reminds him.

From his bag, the inspector takes photocopies and photographs of yellowing documents covered in sloping, pointed, old-fashioned handwriting. The loose pages pile up, slithering over each other and spreading across the table.

'It's a foreign name.'

It pains him to say these words, as if he is leading up to a denunciation.

Jerome isn't listening, his mind is wandering. One sentence catches his attention briefly.

'Your parents had other children before you.'

Jerome screws up his eyes, erases the words as Alexandre says them. His whole body constricts around the stone weighing in his chest, shrinking, growing denser. He tries to concentrate, shakes his head, can't manage it. He hears rustling and creaking. In the distance a Tengmalm's owl hoots.

'Come to the woods,' she sings sadly. 'Come, little boy.'

He answers the call, rolls in the brambles, throws himself down stony banks, crawls under the sheltering bracken, looking for a haven. To hide there, never come out again, forget about daylight and words, growling, ripping things with his teeth, unlearning how to read and write, forgetting everything, staying in peace, alone, in the heart of the forest.

He isn't aware of the noises he's making, doesn't hear the soft, high-pitched moans that his jaws fail to repress.

Alexandre carries on with his report, hands over the story that doesn't belong to him, gets rid of all the inside information, the dealings, the crimes, the victims, the perpetrators, unravels himself – losing his own past and present, his very substance, in the process – until he comes to the acronym, the graveyard name.

'Your parents had six children; they lost six children, and found one,' he says.

On the table he lays out the pages he tore from his notebook. One name on each page, the initial in red: J for Joël, E for Esther, R for Ruben, O for Olga, M for Moshe, E for Elijah. JEROME.

It is the most violent baptism ceremony invented by man since the dawn of time in any corner of the globe.

The letters and numbers rattle around slowly in Jerome's mind, as if in the brain of a halfwit.

He claps a hand over his mouth. Anonymous, he thinks. I've never known who gave birth to me and now even my name doesn't exist. I'm an acronym. I'm nothing. I mean nothing. His blood drains through him like an hourglass. He can feel himself disappearing.

'My mother…' he begins.

'Your mother had four children before the war, with a man called Meyer Abramowicz. They all died, except for her. Your father had two children, and a wife called Rivka Stern. It's all written down. It's your story,' he tells him, putting the black book with red binding into his hands.

Jerome drops it.

'It's not my story,' he says. 'It's nothing to do with me.'

Alexandre looks down. All the same, he thinks, you would have found out eventually with all your digging and scratching at the earth. What have you been looking for all this time? You were haunted. And how couldn't you be? We all are, one way or another, whether we like it or not. It's part of our country, and our generation.

Alexandre remembers his father's diatribes against the Jews. 'Those rats', that's what Cousinet senior used to say. 'Those rats the Jews', who'd ruined everything, corrupted France, stripped it of its honour. Alexandre didn't understand. He was frightened. And what if I'm a Jew too? he wondered. What if I turn into a Jew? How would he know? He prayed timidly not to be one, not to turn into one, or, if it had to happen, for his father not to notice a thing. He's all I've got, he used to think, huddled in his bed. Please let him keep me.

'I've always wondered what it was like to have parents who loved you,' Alexandre says thoughtfully.

And all of sudden, although Jerome couldn't say how or why the movement is reversed, the blood flows back up his arteries, streams through his heart, floods his brain.

We're just probabilities, he thinks. I shouldn't have been born, and I was born. I should have died, and I was saved. His heart thuds in his chest, he can hear it, feel it, as if it were about to leap outside his rib cage.

'I wish I could have come back with some living people for you,' Alexandre continues. 'But that's the problem with this job. The jam jar and everything, that's just to dress it up. The truth is always about death.'

Without admitting it to himself, he was hoping Jerome would feel incredible gratitude towards him, a feeling so strong it would illuminate the rest of his days, an asymptote to passion. But it's the same as usual – once the affair is resolved, the investigator who delved into it is promptly excluded.

Jerome hesitates. He wants to take Alexandre in his arms, to hug him tightly, but he daren't. Gripped by the sort of mawkishness he so loathes, by an emotion he can't deal with, he recapitulates with all his characteristic pedantry, all his crippling idiocy: I've just found out something very important, something very serious. I should be devastated. Anyone else in my shoes would cry and punch the walls and scream. I can't do any of that. My body hasn't got the violence or anger in it. I haven't got the energy.

Jerome thinks of the brave, sturdy baby he once was, tells himself all his strength was used up back then, in the forest, to survive, to believe. Since then, all I've done is accept that I'm here, and that's been enough to wear me out. I don't understand what Alexandre's saying. I don't know why he went off and dug all this up.

While these thoughts painfully form their sequence inside his head, a shape appears, grows, fills the space. The emptiness is still there – that familiar hollow right in the middle of his chest, a heavy stone with nothing around it but the wind – but he's growing in stature, taking on some meaning. Jerome didn't know that his six half-brothers and sisters existed, nor that they'd been murdered. What he has always known, though, is this gap in him, this absence, like an internal echo chamber.

I misjudged you, he wants to tell Alexandre. No one else would have had the courage to go through with what you've done for me. I know how much it pains you. I so badly needed a friend and I've found a brother. But he can't unclench his teeth, because men don't talk to each other like that, because men don't talk to each other.

So he smiles.

21

Marina is first to step off the train, a light bag over her shoulder, her long hair whipped by the wind which rose at the same time as the moon. She smiles at her father, in the halo created round her by the lamp on the platform. She looks like an actor on stage, at the end of a play, waiting for her applause, worn out by her performance, vibrant. As Jerome walks towards her, he can feel his arms coming back to life, growing, spreading like two great wings.

She's changed, like she said in her letter.

It's not the hair, it's something else. Her face is washed, like an Atlantic beach in the spring tides. Her cheeks and eyelids are long and smooth as sandbanks laid bare by the ebbing ocean. She was wrong when she said he wouldn't recognise her. It's the exact opposite. The resemblance between her and himself bowls him over, because it doesn't come from the outside, from the statement bounced back by a reflection, it comes from the inside, from a place somewhere under the skin, the network of muscles that have been permanently imprinted with the stamp of grief. My daughter, he thinks.

In the car, neither of them talks. What can a daughter say to her father? What can a father say to his daughter?

I met Armand a very long time ago, says a voice inside Marina's head. *I was in Year 7 the first time I saw him. And I loved him straight away. I didn't tell anyone, because people think you have to be grown up to feel love, real love. That's not true. But what's the point of making a fuss about that? There isn't any. It was my secret. I loved him straight away because he used to take the side of younger children in fights, and he smiled at me, when he was a big boy in Year 8 and I was just a little Year-7 girl. Armand never looked down on anyone. When I talk about him, people don't believe me, it's like with my love. People have lots of preconceived ideas. They're wary, they want to be right, they're afraid you're making fools of them. If I tell them how kind Armand was, they'll say he was stupid, if I tell them how good looking he was, they'll say he was vain, if I tell them how polite he was, they'll say he was insincere, if I tell them how brave he was, they'll say he was pretentious. So I don't say anything. I didn't say anything before and I won't say anything now. If people need to think that human beings are all self-serving losers and cowardice is the most widespread characteristic in the world, I'll leave them to it. It doesn't bother me. Because I've known love and they can all fuck off. I loved a boy who loved me back. I was lucky to have that and I want to believe that it's like sleeping or an appetite, that it's a gift. He had the gentlest body in the world, but I've never touched another. I'm very knowledgeable and very ignorant. When he died, all life drained out of me. My blood went, along with my tears, and yet I didn't die. I carried on living, with no life inside me. And here I am today. There's no other meaning to this story. If I'm alive, then it's because I'm meant to be. I'm resisting. We're all resisting.*

A voice speaks inside Jerome's head too: *This is the story of a little boy. A baby. That baby is me. I live in the woods, alone. I don't know that there are other babies, not far away, who live in houses. I don't know that they have a mother and a father, brothers, cousins, friends. I'm all alone because my mother's hidden me. My mother has a very gentle voice. I do everything she tells me. I protect her. I take very good care of her. It's easy, all I have to do is listen to her. Quite often she's cold. Sometimes she cries. But I'm never cold and I never cry. I'm the best baby in the world. I'm making this story up because I don't know how it goes. It's true because I'm here, but I don't remember it. I have to make it up, otherwise I don't exist.*

The moon has risen quickly, up and up in the sky, like a great golden biscuit.

'Look,' Jerome says to Marina. 'Look at the moon, how big it is.'

Marina tilts her head to look through the windscreen, and for a moment she rests the side of her head on her father's shoulder.

Keep in touch with
Portobello Books:

Visit portobellobooks.com to discover more.

Portobello